STEPPI

STEPPING OUT

Short stories on friendships between women

Edited by Ann Oosthuizen

LONDON AND NEW YORK

This collection first published in 1986
by Pandora Press (Routledge & Kegan Paul plc)

11 New Fetter Lane, London EC4P 4EE

Published in the USA by
Routledge & Kegan Paul Inc.
in association with Methuen Inc.
29 West 35th Street, New York, NY 10001

Set in 10/13pt Sabon
by Columns of Reading
and printed in Great Britain
by The Guernsey Press Co Ltd
Guernsey, Channel Islands

Library of Congress Cataloging in Publication Data

Stepping out.

1. Short stories, English—Women authors.   2. Women—
Fiction.   3. Friendship—Fiction.   4. English fiction—
20th century.   I. Oosthuizen, Ann.
PR1309.W7S74   1986   823'.01'08353   85-28298

British Library CIP data also available

ISBN 0-86358-048-3

CONTENTS

CONTENTS

ABOUT THE AUTHORS

Honora Bartlett   Honora Bartlett was born in Rochester, New York and now lives in Edinburgh. Her work has appeared in *Spare Rib* and *Time Out* and in American periodicals. She is married to a medieval historian and has a son and a daughter.

Barbara Burford   I am a forty-year-old Black woman, a feminist and a mother of an eleven-year-old daughter. I have had a short story published in *Everyday Matters 2* (Sheba) and was one of the four contributors to *A Dangerous Knowing* (Sheba), a collection of poems by British-based Black women. I was the writer involved in the devised play *Patterns*, which was performed in London in autumn 1984.

Jo Jones   Her daughter writes: My mother spends much of her time in the garden, and then corrects me on the names of the flowers there. She likes reading – as in she 'likes' to breathe. When she isn't in the garden or a book, she is at work, which is in a local school. She has published one novel, *Come Come* (Sheba, 1983), and has just finished another.

Jackie Kay   I was born in Edinburgh in 1961 and brought up in Glasgow. I've had poems published in various magazines including *Artrage* and *Feminist Review*.

A collection of my poems appears in *A Dangerous Knowing* (Sheba, 1984). One of my short stories is published in *Everyday Matters 2* (Sheba, 1984). At the moment I'm writing a novel. Writing is important to me as it's another way of making my dreams visible.

Anna Livia I called my story after Charlotte Mew, for the passion of her poetry, not the pain of her death. I am a lesbian, radical feminist, working at Onlywoman Press, making up stories while I wait for our bike firm to answer their phone. Previously published *Relatively Norma* (Onlywoman), *Accommodation Offered* (Women's Press), various short stories. Forthcoming *Incidents Involving Warmth*, a collection of short stories.

Andrea Freud Lowenstein is the author of *This Place* (Pandora Press), a novel set in a women's prison. She has lived in Cambridge, Massachusetts (USA) for the past ten years, where she founded a community school for women living in a public housing project. She now lives in London, where she is teaching and working on a new novel and a collection of short stories.

Moy McCrory was born in Liverpool in 1953 to Irish parents and grew up in Toxteth attending the local parish church school and later a convent grammar school. She lived for a time in Northern Ireland and now lives and works in London. A collection of her short stories has been published by Sheba (September, 1985) called *The Water's Edge and other stories*.

Sara Maitland is a writer. She was in the *Tales I Tell My Mother* (Journeyman) collective and has since published two novels, *Daughter of Jerusalem* (1978) and *Virgin Territory* (1984); two collections of short stories *Telling Tales* (Journeyman, 1983) and *Weddings and Funerals*

(Brilliance Books, 1984, with Aileen la Tourette) and some non-fiction, mostly about feminist spirituality.

Ann Oosthuizen Her short stories have been published in *Hard Feelings* (The Women's Press) and *Smile Smile Smile Smile* (Sheba). She has been a teacher, a translator (*The Shame is Over* (The Women's Press) and *For Ourselves* (Sheba)), an editor and a publisher. She is a widow with children and grandchildren. She has published a novel, *Loneliness and Other Lovers* (Sheba) and is at present living in Wales and working on her third novel.

Marsha Rowe was born in Sydney, 1944. She worked as a secretary, including two years on the Australian magazines *Oz* and *Vogue*. She left in 1969 to travel. In 1971 she rejoined *Oz* in London and also worked on the underground newspaper *Ink*. In 1972 she co-founded the feminist magazine *Spare Rib*. In 1976 she moved to Yorkshire. She has edited the *Spare Rib Reader* and worked as a freelance writer. In 1980 she had a daughter and in 1983 she returned to live in London.

Michelene Wandor is a poet, playwright, critic and fiction writer. She was Poetry Editor of *Time Out* magazine from 1971 to 1982. Her poetry includes *Upbeat* (1982) and *Gardens of Eden* (1984). Her stage plays are published in *Five Plays* (1984). She writes extensively for radio – plays, features and dramatisations, and her recent work includes *A Consoling Blue* (feature on writer Jean Rhys) and an eight-part dramatisation of Dostoyevsky's *The Brothers Karamazov*. Her book of short stories, *Guests in the Body* is published by Virago (1986). Her history of feminist and gay theatre, *Understudies* is to be published by Pandora Press in autumn 1986.

INTRODUCTION

When I left school, my mother urged me to try to become a member of parliament, but I, a true child of the post-war years, desired only to wear frilly petticoats and bake a chocolate cake. The 'feminine' model I chose seemed to promise a future of certainty and safety – and I had to wait until the 1970s to find a language to express the feeling of suffocation my life produced in me. The knowledge that I was not happy, suppressed because it seemed to deny the love I felt for my family, was linked to a loss of identity, a draining away of any confidence in myself as an individual.

Now, thirty years later, my life is far less fixed. It is as if I am making it up as I go along, so that each day surprises me. I exalt in this new freedom, which I would never again relinquish. I endorse wholeheartedly Simone de Beauvoir's statement of intent, in *The Second Sex*, 'I am interested in the fortunes of the individual as defined, not in terms of happiness, but in terms of liberty,' although I would add my own belief that there is no true happiness without liberty.

And I am certainly meeting women of all ages who seem to be doing the same thing as myself, turning away from constricting models of behaviour, demanding to define themselves. So much so that I have begun to call these women by a special name – I have called them, *the new women*. In spite of a reactionary political climate, a certain set of historical forces has made it possible for women to seize a freedom that they have never before been able to explore in this country. We are, as Honora Bartlett says in her story, 'One of a species who may be getting luckier.'

So when Pandora asked me to edit a collection of stories celebrating the new lives women were leading, and the friendship and support we were giving each other, I was glad to embark on a project of which the concept was not new to me.

I have been able to choose from a great many writers who have been nurtured by women's writing groups and the now robust feminist publishers. Although any collection of short stories reflects the personality of the editor, the selection is of necessity determined not only by its length, but also by the character of individual writers, none of whom will write to order. I had to explain my concept to each one, and hope for the best.

As it turned out, the stories don't follow a particular line. Anna Livia's *5½ Charlotte Mews* and Barbara Burford's *Falling* are love stories. Jackie Kay's *Since Agnes Left* shows a relationship breaking up. I like the fast, tough *5½ Charlotte Mews*, the marvellously romantic *Falling* and the gentle, careful writing of *Since Agnes Left*.

Some Notes on Evolution by Honora Bartlett circles around the misery of a mood and time from which the writer has escaped. *Change your luck*, she urges.

Judy's Kiss by Michelene Wandor lets us into the fun of being in a women's group – not as solemn as the words 'consciousness raising' have made them sound – while at the same time daring, now that we seem to be on safer ground, to describe some of the betrayals we all experienced at the time. The tilt of the story is towards the group, recreating with a kind of *déja vu* all the old 'new ideas', yet blowing them up, so that it brings the past vividly to mind, but with a new edge.

My own story, *A Fine Romance*, is an ironic look at my romance with books. In Marsha Rowe's *Who's she – the cat's mother?* two women imperfectly understand the hidden forces which surface at the birth of a child. Death lurks beneath the bright, fresh descriptions of colour and season.

It's not all easy. In *Strangers* Moy McCrory describes two sisters whose emotions take them to revolutionary action, and then away from it. Not understood, strangers to the families they have nurtured, they lose it all. In *The Mother Right* by Andrea Freud Lowenstein, two women fight for possession of a child. A power struggle, a modern *King Solomon's Ring*, where the tension builds right until the final page, and where the reader, wanting the outcome to be as it is, yet still pities the other woman.

And what collection of stories can do without its witches? In *Superbity* Jo Jones takes a modern look at Jeanette, Saint Joan:

> 'I remember Jeanette who laughed and cried so easily, who won the affections of so many women, loved fine clothes and expected to be honoured, who kept unshakeable loyalty where once she had given it; and in remembering her I find it possible to remember them all. If I knew their names I would sing them. They are reborn in every generation of women, they are alive now, as unmanageable as they ever were.'

Finally, Sara Maitland's *Let us now praise unknown women and our mothers who begat us* celebrates the ordinary, the female, in a fantastic flight over London in a company of women who practise aero-acrobatics, not needing a broomstick, which is completely optional.

I hope these stories will fire the imagination of readers who may be looking for different ways of being in the world, and allow us to explore our new freedom with greater confidence.

Ann Oosthuizen

5½ CHARLOTTE MEWS

Anna Livia

> She sleeps up in the attic there
> Alone, poor maid. 'Tis but a stair
> Betwixt us. Oh! my God! the down,
> The soft young down of her, the brown,
> The brown of her – her eyes, her hair, her hair!
> (Charlotte Mew, *The Farmer's Bride*, 1916)

'Base to Lizzy. Base to Lizzy. Over.'

Middle of New Oxford Street. Damn the bloody radio. Impossible to stop now. Have to edge into the kerb, just when she'd achieved the right-hand lane.

'Base to Lizzy. Base to Lizzy. Crackle. Lizzy, Lizzy, Lizzy. If you hear me, love, give us a couple of rogers. Over.'

Left foot on pavement. Right arm round parcel.

'Lizzy to Base. Lizzy to Base. Over.'

'Lizzy did you pick up at Tiger?'

'Roger. Parcel on Board. Over.'

'POB? Ace. Pick up: Terracotta; Drop: Charlotte Mews.'

'Pick up: Roger. Crackle, crackle Mews?

'Proceed to pick up, then RTB. Over.'

'Roger rog. Over and out.'

Damn and blast. Lizzy did not want to RTB. Not yet. Must be more traffic somewhere. Her daysheet counted 13 drops total. You need at least 15 for breakeven. Kit, the controller, was paying her back. Lizzy was sure of it. Yesterday Lizzy'd totalled 26 drops, no cancellations, no returns, no waiting. Twenty was average for the men, though the longterms expected 30. That's how Fast Buck made money. Kept the multidrops for the longterms, metered the rest out to the bleeps: rarely more than 15 a day. Breakeven. The odd lucky streak thrown in to make you go on playing. Keep your body out of the doorways. Just another way of using it, really. 'Course you weren't meant to know you were being metered. Meant to accept you weren't fast enough, unfamiliar with the streets. Then there was the bleep problem. All you knew was that somebody, somewhere wanted a drop. But to find the pick up you had to dismount, locate a functional phone box, wait your turn in the consequent queue, and ring base. The radios just coasted to the kerb and called in. But a complete set cost £200 so was only allocated to the over 20s. Neat.

Yesterday Lizzy had raced wildly for ten hours in the oozing rain. When you stay wet long enough your rubbers mush, your fingers are anyway too cold to pull the levers and your toes cramp permanently in their clips. Water no longer falls from the sky, but seeps up out of the treacherous earth. Lizzy had crashed reds, let alone ambers; shortcut pavements; been smacked in the mug by a taxi-driver for burning the Wardour one-way. She had literally not stopped all day. Ate a mars bar at Paddington Red Star, but that's all there'd been time for. She wanted to break the 20 a day barrier and achieve a radio. Get up to 30 like the longtermers. Prove she could do it.

Most of the bleeps were women. Fast Buck was an Equal Opportunity Employer. Besides, some firms preferred a pretty packet. Handed you three skimpy slide boxes and asked sweetly, 'Can you manage? We were expecting . . . someone bigger.' Loaded you down with so many videos you thought the *Times* bag would split, then shoved their latest catalogue at you, 'Might as well drop this while you're at it. Saves paying twice.' They liked to think of you weighted down by video nasties, labouring up narrow flights, dropping to their client, a sweating, panting face sandwiched between LESBIAN LUSTS and MEAT CLEAVER FEVER. Cinema drops were the worst. As you chained up you saw the women in hot pants and goose pimples dancing in doorways as if they'd just been walking past, heard the music and were bopping along. While you waited on the buzzer, you could hear them talking to men.

'How 'bout some fun, honey? Want a good time? What do you like? Black, huh, you like black? We got black, we got white, got allsorts. Got anything you want.'

The bleeps rarely mentioned it to each other, but it must happen to all of them. They all had to drop to Soho. Lizzy smiled at the woman dancing. A ghastly smile, knowing that's where she'd end up if she failed at the 15 a day, that's where many of the bleeps came from. Jiggling in a doorway. Though the greenfield drops lent you the ambiguous respectability of the suburbs, when you dragged yourself painting up the steep stairs of Windmill Street, you got to be part of it anyway. That kind of place.

And it slowed you down. 'Lucky little saddle.' 'Try this for thighs.' 'You do go all the way?' 'Nice firm crossbar there between your legs.' Lizzy ignored it, but it slowed you down. Couldn't do a racing start with the men jeering about throwing a leg over. She was fast though. When Kit turned excitedly from the phones and announced, 'Okay, everybody. Seven-minute drop. BJ, you on?' Lizzy was sure she could have done it. Beat a lot of the men anyway on the flat, plus she was a Londoner and hers was a racer. Even the quickest amongst them took ten minutes on a puncture. Lizzy had replaced her wheels with sprints so when she got a flat she just ripped off the old tube and stretched on a new. Two minutes max. Spent the evenings sewing up tyres, but it made the job more lucrative.

The other bleeps were more ladylike than Lizzy. Weren't going to push themselves. Smiled when the longterms asked, 'How many today? Reached double figures?' You got an extra quid waiting time over 10 minutes. The joke went that bleep wages were made up entirely of waiting time. So it was a point of honour not to charge it. Lizzy had sat for over half an hour in an enormous brown leather, open fire office off Saint James's for a bloke to sign his own cheque. Lost two drops just sitting there. 'Mark it down, mark it down,' the secretary hissed as Lizzy scowled. 'Your young men add on at least a pound for every delivery they make.' Lizzy told the other bleeps of her discovery, but they were loth to lose face. The women in Soho still danced in the doorways. Lizzy couldn't see any face to lose. It was a point of honour also to earn as much money as possible. Ever since, Lizzy systematically added a quid per drop.

And now she'd earned a radio. Though there were still problems. The men cut in and ripped off each other's jobs, pretending they'd heard their own name called. More serious, unless she dropped at least 20 today, Lizzy might forfeit the radio. Thirteen down. Another seven to go.

She shot into Percy, dropped the Tiger, leaving her wheels unchained. Should lock up, but no time. Rain'd most probably put them off. Damp saddle. Wet bottom. On to the Terracotta pick up and . . . where was the drop? She could not remember. Mind blank. Panic. Have to radio Base. They'd all hear and Kit would laugh, 'Der, where am I going please, Miss?' in her hoarse whiskey voice.

When Lizzy first rang for a job she was convinced Kit was a man. Then that she was a dyke. Such a deep voice.

She must mean to have such a voice.

'So you wanna work for Fast Buck?' Kit had asked, 'How long you been riding?'

'Since I was 4.'

'Long time. How well d'you know London? The Soho parallelogram?'

'Enough to know it's not one.'

'Unparalleled, huh? Name?'

'Anne Smith.'

'Got one of those already. You'll need a name for the radio.'

Not that Kit planned to give her a radio. Just a new name. It was her who thought up 'Lizzy', 'Lizzy Longacre'. Which, for a 10 hour a day rider, has its little sarcasm.

Kit was a bloody good controller. Six phones at once, 20 riders and never fucked up.

'And if I do, I admit it. That's the first thing. Send the next rider out with a big bottle of whiskey and apologise abjectly. Like this is absolutely unprecedented in the annals of the firm.'

Lizzy wondered why Kit offered her these tips. She was sure as hell never going to work up to controller. Not unless she married, position of trust like that. But at first Kit clearly singled Lizzy out to talk to. Smoothed Lizzy's short, spikey hair so the bristles rubbed her palms silkily; called her hedgehog; told her she was hyper and that was a good thing.

'They say I'm hyper. Only way to be if you got a job to do, and I got 6.'

Lizzy liked Kit. If she worked 10 hours, Kit worked 14. She was there doing the accounts, billing clients, working out daysheets long after the riders had left. She personally checked the radios, re-charged batteries, replaced faulty sets. And she knew the London one-ways like the veins in her wrist. 'Down Dean, up Wardour,' she would remind

Lizzy when Lizzy was offering to burn them, 'Ain't you got no pride?' She never told you wrong addresses, and she always knew what floor. If she and Lizzy had fallen out it was not because Kit metered jobs.

Kit used to help Lizzy. Gave her returns, which doubled your takings if not your prestige. Got her doing paperwork in the slack to round up the pounds. Told her about the old country where it was hot and light. Slowly Lizzy's totals had crept up. 13, 15, 19. So, unlike many bleeps, she didn't pack up the first month in despair.

Then came That Friday. Friday was always worst, because of the weekend looming. Rushes to take to labs, bank drafts to deliver, even contracts to get signed. The funny drops: a piece of liver for the ICA, green test tubes for Regent's Park zoo always seemed to come on a Wednesday, but Friday was one endless scurry. No one took Friday off, not even the newest, most despairing bleep. That Friday was full of panicking bosses sending manic memos to Ms Smith across town, pick ups from one firm only two floors above the drop, but none of their staff could be spared the lift time. Multidrops of urgent minutes going out to 60 Members of the Board. The later it got, the angrier and more abusive were the clients. Lizzy delivered a manilla envelope to an editing firm only to have it ripped up in front of her.

'Tell him it can't be done. It's not reasonable. He simply can't use me like this. Offer a 7 day service, they want it tomorrow. Offer 24 hours, they want it yesterday.'

'Oh they all want it yesterday,' agreed Lizzy philosophically, sensing a return and even a wait during which she could eat her cheese roll.

'Well it's not possible!' shrieked the client in a rage, stamping his foot on the shredded envelope. A comic figure, a clown to amuse other clients with, but Lizzy knew a moment of terrible fear as she glanced at the intercom, checking she knew how to let herself out, away from the crazy.

'Will that be all?' she asked politely, edging for the door. But the man had calmed down, rang whoever and arranged to do the job if Lizzy would wait. Lizzy had now no desire to wait whatsoever but it looked like the only chance she'd have to sit down all day. To refuse a drop was tantamount to resignation and the more tired you were the less likely to look out for side streets, homicidal maniacs, motorbikes cutting you up, the more likely to kiss a juggernaut. The man went off to deal with the editing and Lizzy sank into a deep green sofa, soft enough to cajole the most important client, helped herself to filter coffee and read advertising awards. She gained an hour and a half, only rider to get any break at all, consequently the only one with any speed left in her. Kit's voice on the phone was hoarser and deeper than ever.

About 7 p.m. it began to calm down. Kit sent a couple of longterms out to get crates of beer for the riders. 'Thank you everyone,' she said warmly, 'We've all had one helluva day and I think we've deserved these.' The men knocked back the beer in approval, fizzed it up and frothed it out in a merry shower. Neither Kit nor Lizzy touched the stuff. Kit looked exhausted. On the phone for 15 hours non-stop. Responsible for 20 riders. Hundreds of drops.

'You look dead beat,' said Lizzy, looking at her.

'I am, love, I am,' said Kit, looking back.

'Tough job.'

'Tough cookie!' Kit laughed. 'Could do with a rest yourself.'

'I know,' said Lizzy, 'I'm going greenfields with my girlfriend this weekend.'

And that's when it changed. Kit, with the husky voice, would flirt with Lizzy, of the bristly hair, but if Lizzy was a real dyke Kit didn't wanna know. Or maybe Kit wanted to be butch and Lizzy's sympathy galled. Was it butch to ride flat out and flex your thighs; femme to control the riders, send out for beer for the lads? Sounded right. Only Kit was tall, strong, loud-mouthed and unemotional. Lizzy was little, lithe, nervy and squeaky-voiced. Well, maybe Kit was pissed off Lizzy already had a lover. Not that that should have worried her. They hadn't lasted the weekend. But Kit never said. Just stopped giving Lizzy any but the longest, most arduous drops, up an underpass the wrong side of the motorway. Keep her from central London where the real money was.

On her first day with a radio, Lizzy did not want to call Base for a repeat transmission. She'd done the Tiger, picked up from Terracotta and now where? Oh shit. Return to Base. No chance of another job for half an hour. Put her out of the running. But surely there'd been an address given out before the crackles. Had one of the men cut in on her? Useless as she was POB and they weren't. Lizzy hated to think Kit liked the slimy creatures, called them 'Yes, my sweet,' and 'Yes, my love'. Aberrant to see that big, husky woman with the cheekbones and the jaw chatting up men of all people. The motor bikes in the leather and zips were femme, the pedals, with black tights and condor vests were clearly butch. They were the ones with muscles and a penchant for raw steak. Or perhaps Lizzy's got it wrong again. Couldn't work out butch and femme for women, let alone them.

It was no good. Charlotte Street already and she could not remember the drop.

'Lizzy to Base. Lizzy to Base. Come in Base. Over.'

'Crackle. Crackle. Nyarrzzemd.'

'Lizzy POB in Charlotte Street. Lizzy, Charlotte Street, Parcel On Board.'

'Nyarzz. Static. Splutter.'

'Lizzy? Base here. 5½ Charlotte Mews.'

'Repeat. Repeat drop. Sounded like Charlotte Mews? Over.'

But the radio was dying, if not dead. Trust Kit to give her flat batteries. And she had trusted Kit. Pathetic. But taking directions from Kit used to be pure joy. So beautifully accurate, lyrical almost. 'South along Berwick. West Noel. South Poland. East Darblay. Right at Portland Mews. Yellow doorway, left arch, top buzzer. And return via Hyde. It's hot and you'll like the water fountain.'

Lizzy twiddled the buttons. White noise, more static interference, then:

'Okay everybody, well I'm very pleased to introduce myself. I'm Nyarrzzemd and I shall be one of your 4 encouragers during your time at Charlotte Mews. This is what you might call an orientation speech in which I shall introduce a few basic concepts which may be of use to you in your journey. If you do not feel you can use any encouragement at the present moment, please do not hesitate to turn off. Invert journeyings can be as productive as out and outs.'

Lizzy reckoned she could do with some encouragement. She stayed tuned.

'As you already know, and as we must repeat, our knowledge of your journey is sketchy in the extreme. We cannot advise you concretely except in terms of how best to pit yourselves against adversity. We do not know, however, what constitutes adversity for you. We will ask you to push your muscles to, through, and past breaking point and not break, so that at every moment you are both aching and sinking into pain, transcending pain. You will run till your lungs can no longer gasp, your legs no longer pound nor your feet feel the ground under you. You will swim till your back longs to become a dolphin, or at least a hinge, till the battle to breast the water is almost lost. You will ride till your hands shake and your fingers twitch from clutching, till the ball muscles in your calves harden into marble and your thighs are long, lean tendons of pushing. Only you will know whether you can go on or not, because when you go forth only you will be able to secure yourselves from danger. We will urge you to continue. You must be strong enough to tell us to stop.

'You must prepare yourselves for tremendous depression, also lethargy, fear, misery, confusion, and here we can offer you only exercises in extreme sensory deprivation of a kind you have hitherto not imagined. From what little we know of the journey you are about to undertake, from those few survivors willing to testify, the place to which you are going seems almost to emanate anguish from its roots. These emanations are, of course, traceable to concrete causes by one qualified to judge. You will not be so qualified.

'I hope the following illustrations will give you some idea what to expect of the exercise at least, if not the reality beyond. You are lying in bright sunlight beneath a cloudless sky, the flowers around you the usual mix of azalea translucent and lush tropical. You are thirsty and stand up in search of a glass of water. You go into the house and it's so dark in there after the light outside that you are blinded by the gloom. You can see nothing but walk through the room with your fingertips. Slowly your eyes become used to the dimness and pick out the shadowy outline of familiar objects, begin almost to see a certain beauty in a comparison of greys. Now, hold still at that point. Your eyes, used to the dark, will lose their capacity to appreciate bright colours, will think them gaudy and shy away. Will no longer distinguish between the fresh lime, the deep viridian and the flashing emerald of our native hills. Will call them simply green, tolerate them at dusk only.

'Again, you are lying in bright sunlight beneath a cloudless sky, the sun swarms over your naked body suffusing it with warmth. You feel a slight tightening in your cunt from the simple caress of the sun's rays lazily playing upon it. You do not wish to burn so reach out for some light garment beside you. Slowly, you dress. And with each article of clothing you feel colder and colder and pile on more clothes in search of warmth till, finally, you are muffled under thick sweaters and woollen vests, enormous overcoats and fur-lined gloves, boots on your feet making your steps heavy and awkward, your ears covered in a long knitted scarf so you can scarcely hear. Gone are the bare toes skipping lightly on sand, running luxurious in velvet grass. Now you walk sombrely, and others like you, bumping against each other, hardly hearing and with no idea even of the shape of your own bodies.

'Once more you are lying in bright sunlight beneath a cloudless sky, you are eating peaches. Peaches and cherries, nectarines, plums, tangerines and grapes. They are firm, sweet, soft, juicy, wet. You spit out pips with strong teeth and much laughter. You reach for another. There are none left. There is only custard. Cold custard. Cold, long-congealed and slightly burnt, slightly powdery as though with lumps of mixture not smoothed in. You say you don't like custard. Then there is tinned tomatoes, raw chick peas. You stand up to dance at least if you cannot eat. The band plays a waltz, sweet old-fashioned. You like to waltz but your partner does not keep time and will not touch you, will only jerk spasmodically with grim heroism, hands in pockets. Frantically you look at the pictures on the walls for some soothing symmetry, a flash of energy, a hint of purpose. They are hung slightly crooked. For no reason. It would have been as easy to hang them straight. But they are not. The colours do not clash, they edge uneasily away from one another. There is no vigour in the brush strokes but an apologetic, helpless dash from place to place which peters out ineffectually.

'Finally, across the room you glimpse an old friend, a close friend with whom you have spent long, intense hours talking, persuading, earnestly, happily. You make your way towards her through the heavy, muffled figures in the gloom. You will tell her how it is always cold here, how when the sun shines it is brief and watery, the colours muted and everything tastes of cold, wet custard, slightly sweet. How women dance out of time, the graphics slope off-centre and even the purples and oranges do not clash but sidle. Everything will be bearable if only you two can agree on the clammy, spongelike awfulness. She tells you to cheer up and make the best of it, the cold is not so much harsh as bracing. You'll get used to it, you may even go swimming, give your body to the waves. She giggles. She never used to giggle. She says she likes cold custard, that grey's a very subtle taste, co-ordinates so well with pink. You look out bleakly at the oily sea. She puts a sympathetic hand on your shoulder and tells you you must try to enjoy it a little. You must not feel so passionately; this is a world of men, a world where women care for men, and for men it is neither possible, nor advisable to feel passion.

'Well, this has just been an introductory presentation and I feel it is only fair to ask you all, if only for formality's sake, whether any of you are the least put off by what you have heard. Do please speak now, your niggling doubts, your slightest uncertainties. No one is obliged to go on the journey. So, are you all still committed?

Crackle. Splutter. Criik. Whoosh. Sh, sh. Then another voice began to speak, and another, till there came the sound of many voices speaking together.

'No. No. We're not. Sounds terrible. Perfectly dreadful. Who in her right mind would want to go to a place like that? No wonder they go crazy.'

Then the first voice came back.

'I fully accept your reasoning. Your sentiments are mine exactly. But every generation we have to put the question in case anyone tunes in and feels something is being kept from her.'

Crackle. Crackle. Static interference. And Lizzy's radio fell silent.

'Base to Lizzy. Base to Lizzy. Come in please. Over.'

'Lizzy here. Over,' called Lizzy, dazed at the sound of Kit's voice.

'Current location? You were told to RTB. Over.'

'Sorry, I . . . I . . . Kit, didn't you hear that broadcast?'

'What broadcast? Specify. Over.'

'From Charlotte Mews.'

'Repeat transmission station. Over.'

'5½ Charlotte Mews.'

'I know what it was! Message received and understood. So they're back on air. Has it been that long? There was just a chance with you but you seemed more concerned with drops, I wasn't sure.'

'Unsure of what? Specify uncertainty. Over.'

'That they'd get through to you.'

'To me? They were transmitting to each other. Whole different system. Over.'

'You got tuned, believe me.'

'How do you know? Specify certainty. Over.'

'This journey they were talking about. That's here. I took it.'

'You mean it's not like this there? Weather conditions hot, light, sunny, permanent fixture? Over.'

'Affirmative.'

'So why the hell did you leave, Kit? Weren't taken in by that transcending pain shit?'

'Negative. Kept receiving Outside Broadcasts. Sounded

like a lot of power men had. Deciding, striding, conquering. Hot stuff. Never occurred to me I'd have to be a woman. Over.'

'Women in the Mews don't have power? Over.'

'Affirmative power. Negative work ethic. Over.'

'Negative work ethic? They got no traffic? Over.'

'Double affirmative. Traffic but no deadlines. Love affairs instead. Over.'

'Could speed 'em up. Good love affair.'

'Possibility'.

'Want to try it.'

'Meet you down there, darling.'

'Message received and understood. Proceeding Charlotte Mews. Estimated arrival time 2½ mins. Weather conditions fair to exuberant. Over and Out.'

SOME NOTES ON EVOLUTION

Honora Bartlett

On the tenth anniversary of the summer of 1968, the newspapers were full of the published memories of radicals, memories of Paris and Chicago and the LSE. Betsy would pick up these newspapers and see the date in big numerals running across the top of the page and try to remember these things. But what she saw, when she closed her eyes, was herself in 1968. Still in America, still a student; not yet twenty years old. A strange little figure, but how familiar.

Politics seemed to her then as shadowy as the photographs in newspapers could make them. Her intenser life was elsewhere. In 1968 she was hardly thinking of those big events, though of course she talked about them, she had opinions. She can almost remember some of her opinions. But there are other things about that time which come to her without effort, whether she wants them to or not. Her own real memories of 1968.

It is more than ten years ago now. And if the possibility of a General Strike in France will not occur again in quite the same way, there are other and different things that will not happen again either.

Many of her friends long for the sixties. They cast loving looks over their shoulders at that lost time, they would like to relive it. Not Betsy. She does not want to go back.

A little while ago she overheard a conversation in

which a young philosophy professor was saying that philosophers have never been able to answer the question of why time should proceed as it does in a forward direction. It is a much-debated subject: no one can explain why it happens that way, and no one can prove that it will continue to happen. Though of course there is no good reason to believe that it will not.

Betsy wants to protest when she hears this, she wants to scream. She presses her lips together and thinks, she would keep time moving forward, if only by the force of her own will. She believes in progress. She is not nostalgic. She will never go back.

The things that used to happen to her cannot happen to her again.

She will never again sit, lovesick and sullen, on the edge of one of Professor Ramjee's wicker chairs, lifting her eyes only to intersect the looks he directs at her friend Susan.

Susan did not want to return those looks. She talked, animated by the knowledge that she was admired as she spoke, to Ramjee's English wife. She had her cornered on the sofa and was sitting very close to her, with her head tilted to one side so that her hair almost brushed the other woman's shoulder. Mrs Ramjee hardly seemed to notice: she sat drinking vermouth with her thin legs folded up under her like an insect's and her eyes fixed in courteous misery on Susan's. Just occasionally, when Ramjee was talking to Betsy and Susan was momentarily silent, his wife would flick a sudden, frightened glance over at him. She never looked at Betsy. Only at Susan and Ramjee.

Susan's one source of unhappiness that summer was that Mrs Ramjee could not love her too. She brooded over this. It was inconvenient, for they had to spend so much time together. And Susan liked love. The whole world was calling out to her with its love – every day there were letters and telephone calls, from New York, from Boston, all saying, *Come, Susan, please come* – but she wanted more of it. And why not? Why wouldn't this woman like her? She was no threat. She would not have a love affair with her husband. She avoided his searching looks.

Did Ramjee know all along that Susan was never going to sleep with him? Betsy wondered.

She knew, by then. She knew as well as she knew anything that summer that Susan was never going to sleep with her again.

'Poor Betsy. How ever am I going to comfort you?' she had said laughing, the first time. Beautiful girl, perfect girl. Perfect life. Her parents' summer house, where they slept, but not together, blinked lights at the Ramjees' little cottage from across the Bay. Did Ramjee walk out to watch the lights, like Gatsby, on the evenings he didn't see her? Probably. American literature was his subject, after all.

The last night they were all together Betsy woke suddenly out of the stupor engendered by hopeless love to observe that he was insulting her. He was saying terrible things to her. Perhaps he'd been doing it all summer, and she hadn't seen it. Perhaps he'd spent six weeks heaping insults on her, on Betsy, his bright student.

She sat, mute as a baby but not uncomprehending, while his words fell around her: *Why have you stayed so long? You said two weeks.* And Susan, a little drunk by then, gravelly-voiced and slyly sweet to both of them, elected to ignore all this. She didn't like to recognise these things. Betsy didn't either. But that night he said when she was leaving – suddenly his hostility erupted and in the gentlemanly act of putting her into her car he snarled – *Go back to your West.*

It took her a moment to think what he meant, and then she saw: he wanted her to go home, to retrace her steps, to go back where she belonged. As if she belonged there.

She wanted to say something back to him, something

witty and historical about how she couldn't do that any more, about how the frontier was closed and it was no longer the land of opportunity. She wasn't ready to cry yet, but something swarming at the back of her throat made her want to sting him. Instead she said, pretending it was a normal exchange, or, as he would say, with his Anglo-Indian perversity, a *not abnormal* exchange, 'Actually, we're going to New York tomorrow. Both of us,' she added, smiling up at him full of malice. 'Both of us.'

Did she really say it twice? It was the way she remembered it. But perhaps she was not that heavy-handed, even then.

And perhaps he knew it already. He turned without speaking and walked back into the cottage. How straight his back was, how stiff. And Susan came right after her, was getting enigmatically into bed a few minutes later. Betsy tried to laugh at Ramjee – his last chance gone. But the soreness that his insult, his many insults, had left was beginning to penetrate her thoughts, and she lay going over and over it, rubbing it back and forth like toothache. In the morning she felt as if she had been kicked and beaten.

How very much he had wanted her out of his house. And it was not just because she was extra, an unwanted chaperone. It was not that. His malevolence was directed against her. He saw her, not Susan, not his wife, as the source of his predicament.

He knew that she and Susan had been lovers then – perhaps. Once during the evening he had spoken to her about some lesbians he had met. He called them 'a select': one of his strange terms, a term that she had never heard before but at which her eager snobbery pricked its ears. As he had doubtless known it would. He said, *I could give you the address*.

When she had been away from America for a few years

she would still find herself sometimes thinking of writing to Ramjee to say, 'Don't worry, Susan has such a cold heart, she could never love anybody.'

But even then she did not know if that were true. Susan got married in Paris in 1970: lovely wedding, lovely husband. At the wedding Betsy seemed to be watching them both from a great distance, though in fact she was standing up very close. She was hugged many times by both bride and groom, and groom in particular was attentive to her. They got on well, but she went away unable to think about him. She could not say anything to herself about him.

And then he died. He had been dying all the time; all the time he was standing up straight and smiling and having his picture taken with Susan, a little, quiet process had been going on in his body, a process that could not be reversed. Betsy, hearing about it in a letter from Susan's sister, carried around with her for days an image out of an old biology textbook; the little army of white blood cells, surging supportively around the red. But in his case they had not, they had mutinied. A few months after the wedding he was dead.

And when he died Susan was undone. No one could help her. Betsy had lunch one day with their old friend Jean who said, 'Susan is like a zombie since Finn died.' And Betsy, angry, frightened at the thought that Susan might have changed altogether, said, 'She always was a zombie.'

Someone else at the table laughed. But Jean made her eyes very round and said, 'Betsy, you are extraordinary. You don't care for anyone. You only care whether you can get a good joke out of them.'

'No!' *No, no.* That wasn't it at all. Tears gathered in her eyes at such an accusation. She loved Susan. Susan had never loved *her.*

She and Professor Ramjee had this in common. Perhaps

that was it, that was why he hated her. And he did: for a year, when Susan had already graduated and gone away to Paris, he was still Betsy's teacher. And for a year her knees buckled under her whenever she had to approach him to talk about Emily Dickinson. His fury had hidden itself; now he was noncommital. 'All right, all right,' he would say, when she fished an idea up from her notes and held it out, pleadingly, to him. He would rest his forehead on his beautiful hand and look down again at the papers he was correcting. Betsy would hover awhile, then slink away.

That year, her last year in America, was a ruin. She had spent three years in a state of grace miraculously preserved, and she fell from it utterly. The laws of evolution which had been tenderly governing her progress had turned themselves around, and she felt herself losing the faculties she had developed for climbing. She was changing into an eely creature, helpless in a slippery world. She could not find a hold anywhere.

She had to run away in the end, to England. At least she could do that. She had to try for a second chance, to begin all over again in a new place.

She went first to Oxford, driven by the same eagerness for a particular kind of achievement that had propelled her through university in America, before she began to run down.

When in her memory of that time she saw herself coming to England it was as though she had run all the way. It was such a long time before her breath came back to her.

At some moment in the two years she spent in Oxford she began to observe how men and women take part in many processes at once. In America she had been too preoccupied with her own efforts to rise out of nonentity to perceive that they took their place in a larger set of movements.

She looked and saw that all around her there were people who had made themselves up, as she had, almost out of nothing. The private striving that had so organised and dominated her life in America seemed in Oxford to be a general, a public thing. Everyone was trying to get somewhere.

She pulled away from it a little then. She began to regard her life not as a race to be run but as a problem to be solved. 'Politics' began to seem like a different kind of word.

She remembered that Ramjee had been to Oxford, too, ten years earlier. Where he would have been, not a sleek and powerful male among others, but a talented freak, like Jaris, the young Indian man who was her tutorial partner. There were certain signals – the sudden switches from staggering charm to timidity, from timidity and charm to hard undisguised self-interest – that she grew to recognise as the rhythmic output not of arrogance but of cultural hysteria.

Betsy knows such a man now, in London: he grew up in India and then made his way, as she did, to England, 'to complete his development'. He is pleasant and intelligent, with an entirely beautiful English wife; and he tells Betsy how the colonial male's experiences are not unlike those of women. The colonial sees himself observed, measured, imprisoned by the categories of the imperial culture which dominates him, but to which he will never measure up, never exactly correspond. Like a woman, he sees his behaviour as a composite exhibit, a series of snapshots or studies of face, voice, manner, to be taken and kept in the files of an endless relay of smooth golden ex-public school boys who sit smiling quizzically not only from behind big desks in high-ceilinged rooms, but in the mind, in the mind, too.

He tells her that he too knows what it is to be patronised. To sit on the edge of his chair.

Like Ramjee he has wonderful, eyes, dark-ringed. He takes off his glasses and rubs his eyes with the square tips of his long fingers. His beautiful wife smiles, watching him, and leans across the table to stroke his cheek. Her hands are startlingly schoolgirlish by contrast; short, pale, bitten. It makes an intriguing picture.

Betsy likes to watch them together; but she pays attention also to his analogy. It is not complete, not by any means. They have been through quite different processes.

He does not mention the women of his country, and Betsy notes this silence. It is like the silence of those women's individual lives, so unrecorded. Even by this man, who is so sensitive to social injustice, who has so much data of his own.

His sisters are not in London, nor the daughters of his sisters' servants. Development begins from different points, and takes people to very different places. This is what Betsy thinks about much of the time. This is what she calls politics.

What does the man's word 'development' mean, to the women of his father's large household in a village near Bombay? Do they think of going one day to a university far away, or do they think of walking one morning down the village's main street by themselves, without father or brother or male cousin to guide them?

As for herself, Betsy cannot quite believe the lingering touch of the luck which set her going in 1948 in a clean Catholic hospital in Tacoma, Washington. The lives of most women, of most of the women who have ever lived, hover over her like the shadow of a big bird, with talons. She feels herself to be a very small animal, but lucky: one of a species that may be getting luckier.

Still she shivers: the shadow is very close. The sufferings of other women move her to tears and to anger, but she is glad that she has always known when to run.

She likes her beautiful friend's Indian husband, but it does not occur to him to notice the women of India even while he is working so hard to recommend himself to her. She thinks he might be something of a sexist. In 1968 the word 'sexist' did not exist, or if it did Betsy did not know it. She knew what it was, though, to sit among her male professors, talking away like the child Jesus in the temple, and then suddenly to know that she had been talking too long, that the space left in their conversation for the speech of women had been filled and that she had begun to overspill it. It was as though a small receptacle was provided for her which gave her words shape and made them worthy of attention, but when she had filled it she began to talk loosely, her effects began to run away from her like tepid water out of the sides of an old bath. The men grew impatient. When she awoke to this she would fall silent. She would not even finish her sentnece. She hoped no one would notice; and no one did. The conversation had already called 'next'. It was some man's turn to talk.

Those bruising awakenings. Surely they are over now? Surely the world has altered, or her segment of it has, and she will never again sit up suddenly to find herself in the comany of that male determination to exclude her, as the author can, from his play.

Women might do that still; write her in, write her out. But it is different. When women live as adults but without men, without families, they are deprived of some of the weapons to which, in other situations, they adapt. When so much energy is spent on fashioning a new habitat, there is not so much left over for the devices of the old.

The women Betsy knows now spend a lot of time proposing new standards – of behaviour, ethics, style. She does this also. No one can meet them. But the standards are out in the open. They can be described, they can be explained. Betsy hugs this to herself like an amulet. It is this explicitness that is the law of her new world.

For her, it is no longer the way it was in 1968, when Susan's family watched her from their distance, when they hissed sourfaced as she passed out of the dining room, *What is wrong with that girl?* They knew she could hear them. They wanted her to hear that they knew what was right for Susan, and that she wasn't right.

Their standards were something she had heard about from the beginning. Susan made fun of them, but as of something real and absolute, like the Flag. Betsy was never wholly certain what these standards were. But she knew as well as they did how far short of them she must fall. The old lady, the grandmother, said one day to Susan, 'Your sister is too snobbish, but you are not snobbish enough. That girl can do nothing for you.' *Nothing*.

Susan repeated this gaily. A joke. Silly Grandma. Silly Mummy and Daddy. 'They don't know you.' She gave Betsy a glancing kiss.

But by then they were no longer lovers. *How can I comfort you?* was the thing she first said, leaning forward to tuck some short hair back behind Betsy's ear, letting her hand just stay there, light as a bird, for a second.

But she gave no comfort. Not in the end. 'I think you should go home now,' she said quietly, lying quietly in her bed. And then, quickly, to follow it up, the honest simple superior young woman again, 'I mean, I have to get a job for awhile before I go to Paris. I can't just entertain all summer.' She went to sleep then, her burden lifted from her.

Betsy got up and packed her bags. She did not get a job when she went home. She lay all summer in her parents' back garden with her eyes shut against the sun, lay there every day until she felt sick and her back was wet and marked with the weave of the hammock.

Her parents didn't know what was wrong with her,

either. But they were Catholics and they were lower-middle-class and they had lived all their lives in the West. Betsy had spent three years very far away from them, it was a long way across the continent to her college and to the houses where she had spent her holidays. Her parents didn't ask her many questions any more. In the afternoons her mother would bring her tea, and she was grateful and drank it.

She pretended sometimes that they had asked her what was wrong, and she tried to think what she would say. 'I'm dying of a broken heart,' she thought, almost speaking aloud. Or: 'I'm dying of shame.'

When she came back to college she had a good tan, but it was not enough to protect her. The year passed with terrible speed. She ran and ran to keep herself from falling into the deep hole that had been prepared for her. She finished her work for Professor Ramjee; at any rate she brought it to an end. She passed her exams. She had the last conversations she would ever have, with people she had once thought she could never bear to leave. The cloud that attended her movements was real, but she kept herself from disappearing into it utterly, as she had already seen others do; even then, when they were all so young. Her sweet friend Phoebe, her first lover, had begun to die of something like this, of shame or a broken heart, and she was still dying, sitting in her apartment in Boston, drinking beer and watching television and mourning herself and dying, and she would not rise again. But Betsy refused to be compelled to such deaths. She refused even to attend them. She went away.

'Start again in a new place,' she tells her friends in London when things go wrong for them. 'Change continents.' *Change your luck*.

She thinks of herself as an animal who has so far survived a very dangerous process: and she considers herself lucky, for personal survival is only one of a very wide range of possibilities. Often she is surprised at her own success.

She is past thirty now. Even among such unhandy primates as men and women, thirty years signals full adulthood. She has grown up and the world has moved forward. The sorrows of the past are not hard to remember, but from where she is now it seems that nothing so sad can ever happen to her again.

FALLING

Barbara Burford

'Oh my god!'

Alison could no longer pretend enough to sit calmly drinking her coffee.

'Why did you do it?' she asked herself, leaning her forehead against the cool glass of the kitchen window. 'What did you have to go and do it for?' She began to pace up and down the narrow galley kitchen, dire visions of two people trying to cope in this space, crowding into her mind.

'Why don't you come and stay with me?' she mimicked herself in facilitating mode. And remembered how Joan's eyes had widened momentarily; the shock there, before the mask had come down, and Joan had tried very carefully to back out. But all the other women had been so enthusiastic. This was what sisterhood was about: sharing, facilitating. It was all so beautifully simple for them. Reaffirming. Joan had been accepted on a course in London, but couldn't find accommodation: Alison had her own flat there and was offering to put her up. Great! It had been settled over their heads.

She paced out of the kitchen and into her tiny hall. She had been so proud of her newly acquired flat; achieved after years of scrimping, saving, making do with other people's rooms and furniture.

'Look at what you've been and gone and done,' she said woefully to her reflection in the mirror. It wasn't as if she knew the woman, really knew her. They'd been meeting for years at various conferences and meetings up and down the country. Usually head-on. Arguing fiercely, getting as high as kites on each other, and making no attempt outside these times to meet or correspond. Yet she now realised that for her a conference only really took off when she spotted Joan in the registration-greeting-mêlée that began these affairs. Joan, eyes flashing, teeth shining against her black skin as she kissed and hugged friends. Never Alison though. Between them it was usually a carefully casual, 'Hi!' and some banal comments, generally about problems of getting to the conference. Now she found herself wondering if Joan had found the conference that she had missed because of flu as flat as she had found the one in Nottingham that Joan had not attended.

She opened the door of the room that she had planned to have as her study. She had got as far as buying a secondhand desk and chair, but had been saving up to buy the wood for shelving. Beech, she had thought, imagining all her books collected in this one room, covers glowing enticingly against the pale wood. She'd be able to get some real writing done at last, produce some really stunningly reasoned papers for conferences, instead of the notes hastily scribbled the night before, that she usually relied on. The secondhand divan had put paid to the shelves for the next few months. But then her study was going to be Joan's room for the next ten weeks. True, Joan had said not to bother about a bed, that she'd be quite happy rolling up in her sleeping bag on the floor. But Alison had taken one guilty look at her own oversprung mahogany monstrosity last weekend after Joan's call, and had gone out and bought the divan and some bedding to go with it. After all, it would be useful if she had others to stay.

Suppose she doesn't turn up? thought Joan, easing the weight of her rucksack on the ledge behind her. I could phone her. But suppose she's not there? Suppose she's there, but pretends to have forgotten that it's today, or something like that? What do I do then? No way that I'm going to force myself on her. It's bad enough as it is. I'm sure she didn't mean it. But the others took it out of her hands; out of both our hands. I'd only intended to make a point about class and privilege. About some women not having real access because of lack of amenities. Not being able to take up my place on this course because I couldn't afford London accommodation prices seemed a good example. And then Alison had to come the great white benefactress.

She'd meant to let her off the hook later, was sure that she would have found somewhere else before the date, but nothing had come up. And this course was too important to miss.

Gloria! Gloria would give her a space to sleep. But she couldn't stay there for long. Gloria and her child only had a bedsitter. How long would it take to find somewhere else? Somewhere she could afford. Where she could do all the studying that she would need to do to keep up after all these years of not studying full-time. Maybe it would be easier on the spot. She couldn't go back to Birmingham. She'd given up her place. Couldn't afford to keep it on, her things farmed out to friends.

'Oh shit!' she twitched her shoulders where the rucksack straps were pulling, and looked at the clock again. She felt itchy and overheated in her heavy duffel coat, but it was easier to wear it than to carry it.

'Hi! Sorry I'm late. Murder trying to find somewhere to park.' Alison stood in front of her, beautifully turned out in a green track suit, not a hair out of place, glasses twinkling. 'Shall I take these?' She reached for the two holdalls at Joan's feet and staggered a bit at their weight.

'I'll take one. They're full of books.' They tussled politely and decided to share the weight of one between them. It didn't really work because Joan was taller and, weighted as she was by the rucksack, leaning over threw her slightly off balance. They negotiated the big doors out to the front of the station and staggered across the forecourt to the road.

'Look, you wait here, and I'll fetch the car.' Alison turned to Joan. 'You must be exhausted. Let me help you off with your rucksack.'

'S'okay. I can manage. You go ahead.' Did Alison think that she'd worn her rucksack all the way from Birmingham, or something? She watched her dart across the road. All that energy. Lately Joan had felt exhausted all the time. She'd have to find some energy somewhere if she was to survive the next ten weeks.

Alison stopped talking and concentrated on the traffic instead. Joan was obviously not with her. There was nothing here of the laughing, animated, argumentative woman she remembered. This tall, quiet, withdrawn black woman slouching in the seat next to her seemed even more of a stranger. She had meant to point out various things to Joan: the health-food co-op; the post office; the nearest tube station; but she held her peace. It wasn't an uncomfortable silence. Just strange. Other. She found herself fighing two contrary impulses. One to rile Joan by flying some politically right-off verbal kite; and the other, to pat Joan's shoulder and say something truly daft like, 'There, there,' or, 'It's okay.' Instead she pulled up in front of the flat and said brightly, 'Here we are!' and was out of the car and opening the boot before Joan had climbed out.

'Sorry. Not with it,' Joan said. 'No sleep last night.'

Probably for the same reason I didn't, Alison thought

grimly, then went scarlet as another reason flashed through her mind in full technicolour. She ducked her head quickly inside the boot.

Help! Where did that come from? Lucky Joan, at least she didn't go beetroot for all the world to see. Then she caught herself. Lucky Joan? How could she be lucky being black? But Joan was proud of being black. Everything about her said so. She realised Joan was standing with the rucksack and one bag, waiting for her.

'Sorry. Wool-gathering,' she tried to say lightly, and busied herself locking the car.

'Looks more like a brown study to me,' Joan said, and regretted it instantly at Alison's controlled flinch. She dropped the bag and spoke to Alison across the car roof. 'This is a very bad idea.'

'No don't say that. It's a very good idea. It's just that ideas and reality are a bit different . . .'

'And this right-on idea is suddenly standing here as large as life and twice as . . .'

'Look, let's not quarrel in the street. Let's go inside and have some tea. We have to talk. I can see that.'

'If another white woman says to me in that unctuous sincere tone "We have to talk" . . .' then Joan realised that she had actually spoken aloud. 'I'm sorry. I shouldn't have said that. I'm very tired and a bit strung up. It's no excuse really . . .'

'Let's go indoors,' Alison managed to speak calmly. Inside she was shaking as if she had just narrowly avoided an accident in the car.

'Coffee? Or there's some wine.' Alison made herself turn to face Joan who was leaning against the kitchen window sill, looking so impermanent that Alison wondered how she would get her to stay. She wanted her to stay, she knew that now. And not, she hoped, just because of the repercussions, the comebacks if it ever got out to other women.

'Not wine. Coffee would be fine.' Joan looked back directly at Alison. 'I haven't eaten – and that's not a hint – but I think I'd better have a clear head. I'm feeling very defensive, and when that happens I usually attack. Not good.' She shook her head wryly.

'I go quiet and brood.'

'A lot safer.'

'But, I'm told, very angry-making.' She finished the preparations with the coffee maker.

'To tell the truth, I never expected to be here. I thought that something else would come up.'

'And it didn't?' Alison was unreasonably hurt by this quiet statement. Hadn't she been hoping that Joan would make other arrangements?

'Nothing suitable. And this course is too important to miss. Maybe now I'm down here, I'll be able to find somewhere else.'

'I offered to put you up for the full ten weeks, you know. I'll understand if you want to find somewhere else, but . . .' her voice trailed off. She wanted to say that Joan was very welcome to stay, but realised in time the polite emptiness of the words.

'I know you did, but admit it you were guilt-tripped into it.'

'No I wasn't. I offered.'

'Yeah. But I don't think you expected me to take you up on it.'

'I meant it.' Alison decided to be brave. 'But you were really shocked. Why?'

A quick sideways flick of the eyes from Joan, and then her face became very still. But she didn't deny Alison's statement. Alison poured them both coffee and set sugar and milk on the table between them. She sat down.

'Why?' Alison repeated the question.

Joan didn't sit down or reach for her coffee. It was as if, Alison thought, she couldn't bear to even symbolically break bread with her. She got up and fetched some biscuits. When she turned back Joan was looking down, and she couldn't read her expression.

'How long have we been meeting each other at conferences, Alison?'

'Years I suppose.'

'Yet you know nothing about me, and I know nothing about you. We're strangers.'

'That's not true. I know how you feel on a lot of issues, I know your politics.'

'But you don't know me. And you weren't interested in knowing me.'

'I would have liked to, I think, but . . .'

'You think!'

'Oh, come on! You never made any moves towards me either, you know. You're very difficult to approach – you make it very difficult. What could I have said? What could I have done? You always seemed to be with the other black women at the socials.'

'And you were always with the white women.'

'Well, where the hell else could I go? What was I supposed to do? Drag you away by the elbow? And say what? "We have to talk!"?'

'You had my phone number, my address, on the contact sheet.'

'Dammit! You had mine too!'

'Touché!' Joan acknowledged wryly.

'Are you still trying to pick a fight, Joan? Because I think that's what you're doing, have been doing since I picked you up.'

'True.' Joan at last sat down and reached for her coffee. 'One thing I learned very early on, when I was a small child, was that anything that I wanted so badly that it put me in suppliant position, I had better not want. Because I always found the price too high.'

'I offered. You didn't even have to ask. Try and

remember that.'

'Stop being so damned patronising.'

'Stop being so bloodyminded.'

'It was just so public. As if you wanted to score a few right-on points.'

'Yeah, and if I'd come up to you afterwards, always supposing I could get near you, and asked you privately, you would have thought it was because I didn't want anyone to know. It was an impulse, and I think a true reflection of what I felt. Don't ask me why. I saw your need, and I wanted to help.'

'And you're going to tell me you've had no regrets.'

'Not regrets. I don't know how to describe it. Qualms maybe. You're so hot on class and race issues, and you'd be right here, in my home, judging me . . .'

'The private face of the white middle-class liberal?'

'Something like that.'

Joan began to laugh, and on seeing the outrage on Alison's face laughed even harder.

'It's not funny. This morning I felt I'd even have to police my mind, watch what I thought. You've no idea how strange it felt.'

'No.' Joan was suddenly serious. 'That's a luxury I don't have. The choice. Not with all the negative junk that comes at me from every direction.'

'I won't insult you by saying, I know. And I won't ask you to teach me either.' Alison looked steadily back at Joan.

Joan drank her coffee and ate a biscuit, and Alison found herself doing the same. Then Joan stood and walked round the table to stand by Alison. 'Hi, Alison.' She smiled down at her. 'Thank you for offering to put me up.' Alison smiled back a trifle uncertainly, not really sure that Joan was going to stay even now. 'Where shall I put my stuff?'

Joan woke early, her body feeling like wet mush. She'd have to do something about this divan. Too soft, too saggy. She smiled to herself as she remembered Alison's guilty explanations as to why she'd bought it. At least she'd been honest. Her muscles had protested at the sight of Alison's mahogany marshmallow. God, she must need a snorkel to sleep in that!

She lay for a moment in the quiet Sunday morning warmth of the flat, absorbing the sounds: the minute crackling of the radiator, the rather half-hearted trial runs of birdsong from beyond the curtains. She felt Alison's presence, or more precisely was aware of her as a sifting essence, as much a part of the room, with its strong clear colours, as the slats of pale spring sunlight fingering between the curtains.

'Enough already!' she muttered and heaved herself out of bed, swearing as the rug slipped slightly on the polished floorboards. 'You will have to go,' she addressed its faded intricacy. 'You're beautiful, but I don't need any broken bits right now.' She rolled it up and stowed it in a corner. She located her warm underthings and got dressed, appreciating the rising heat from the radiator. A few gentle stretching exercises to loosen her up, then she pulled on her tracksuit, found her shoes and the key, and let herself quietly out of the flat.

Alison heard her leave and leapt out of bed to peer through the net curtains, just in time to see Joan easing herself into a run. Probably heading for the park, she thought, admitting her relief. For a moment she had expected to see Joan and her bags disappearing up the street. It was the same relief she'd felt when on returning last night she had seen the thread of light under Joan's closed door.

'Joan's door, eh?' she asked herself quizzically before getting back into bed.

The others had wanted to come back for coffee last

night, wanting obviously to view the new exhibit, but she'd found herself using Joan's plea of tiredness for not asking them in. For, let's face it, she could not have guaranteed that Joan would have been there to view. Imagine what Anthea, Wendy, and especially Esther would have made of the, no doubt polite, note that Joan would have left. Alison had sighed with relief in the hallway when she'd seen that thread of light.

She snuggled back down into bed. Sunday morning . . . lovely. . . .

Alison surfaced again to the sound of the shower, and was instantly aware of an urgent need to pee. She tensed all her thigh muscles and tried to ignore the sound of rushing water. Stupid arrangement, having the loo in the bathroom.

Please, let her not be a dawdler! Why don't I just walk in there and pee? She's a woman, so am I. Why can't I?

Aeons later, it seemed, the shower stopped and Alison slid sideways out of bed, muscles clenched. Joan still hadn't come out of the bathroom. What if I pee myself? She stifled a giggle that threatened her control; then caught sight of herself in the mirror – starkers, all sleep-crumpled. She didn't even have a robe.

Bloody Joan Fisher!

Alison pulled on a tee shirt but didn't have the control for knickers. Joan's door closed quietly and Alison shot into the hall, and barely reached the loo.

The relief! She muttered, 'We have to talk . . .' then, 'Reclaim the loo!'

Back in her room she debated getting dressed or just putting on some trousers. She decided finally on a defiant note, and put some knickers on. After all, she paid the heating bills so she could relax when she was at home. She fetched the papers from the letterbox and strode into the kitchen. Joan, damn her eyes, was spruce in jeans and a clean shirt, and was halfway through a bowl of cereal. She looked up but didn't smile or speak.

'Morning,' Alison muttered aggrievedly, missing Joan's raised eyebrow, as she turned on the grill and contemplated the full coffee pot. Full of Joan's coffee. She clattered around making toast. How the hell was she to get round that one? Although they were both vegetarians they'd decided yesterday to each be responsible for their own food, and Joan had gone shopping.

When Joan spoke behind her, she jumped. 'What?'

'Perhaps it would be a good idea to pool the coffee supplies.'

'Oh?' God, Joan moved quietly. 'Yes . . . yes! Good idea.' Alison wanted to scream. 'Thanks.' She accepted a cup of coffee instead.

Up close, Joan smelt of baby lotion and shampoo, and tiny glints of water were trapped in the intricate curls of her hair. Like dew in a spiderweb, Alison thought, and sat down facing the wrong way, because Joan was in Alison's usual chair.

Joan drank her coffee, then poured herself another cup.

'You want a bit of this?' Alison offered Joan the review section.

'No thanks, never use them.'

Alison lit her first cigarette and glared defiantly at Joan. Joan smiled and reached for an apple.

I hate you, Joan Fisher, Alison intoned inside. And I'm not going to get dressed, or even clean my teeth, till I'm ready.

'What?' Joan asked round a mouthful of apple.

'I didn't say anything,' Alison tried to sound preoccupied.

'You have a very loud smoulder.'

Alison thought of a quote from Rita Mae Brown, she of the epic insults. 'Piss on your teeth,' Joan Fisher! She smiled beatifically at Joan.

She looks like a hen, thought Joan. Atilla The Hen. And coughed to cover a laugh. That, she could see, made Alison madder, for she blew a defiant plume of smoke into the air. Joan felt good, connected. The run in the park had lifted her. She felt the tensions in her muscles, shifted her bare feet on the floor. She wanted to dance. Later she would. Right now she was getting an unholy enjoyment out of Ms Volcano opposite. It was a wonder the newspaper didn't start to char at the edges.

God, she was being unfair to Alison. She really should leave her to her bad mood. She should not disseminate her own good vibes in a row. Plenty of time for that over the next ten weeks. She stretched luxuriously into the sunlight, rocking her chair back.

Alison snorted and the paper sounded in imminent danger of dismemberment.

Music, Joan thought. What would she use this morning? Something slow, intricate, peaceful. Then she remembered: she'd been too tired to check with Alison yesterday once she'd realised that the flat was on the first floor. Bloody Alison, who'd never once asked her what her course was about. Shit! She really needed to dance, particularly before she hit the books this afternoon. Besides, three days without dancing, then having dance and movement classes first thing tomorrow, along with everybody else. Perhaps there would be somewhere at the Centre that she could use early in the morning or even after hours. But today, now, there were so many things, emotions, boiling inside her that could only be sorted or stilled in the dance. She let the chair rock gently back onto four legs.

'Alison . . .' she began.

'OK! I give in!' Alison replied, folding the paper. 'I know I should have; and I was going to; but every time, something else came up, and we'd be off again.'

Weird, Joan thought. But it had sometimes got like that

when they were arguing in workshops. Like two-handed verbal hop-scotch. And then they'd leave everybody else behind.

'Dance as therapy,' she said, watching Alison mercilessly.

'Dance as therapy.' Alison tasted the words, trying to match them up with her image of Joan. The one she kept in the top right-hand side of her mind. What? She tiptoed hastily away from that.

'But you don't dance!' she exclaimed, covering her mental tracks quickly. 'I've never seen you dance.'

'You've never seen me ride a bicycle either.'

'What's that got to do with anything? I was just saying that at all those socials, I've never once seen you dance.'

'That's not dancing. That's posing to music.'

'Oh, come on! I won't let you get away with that one. What I see is a lot of women having a good time together. Just because you don't indulge in something, doesn't make it invalid.'

'Did I say that?'

'You implied it.'

'Rubbish. . . .'

'Hold it!' Alison slapped the table, startling them both. 'I've never known anyone like you, Joan, for red herrings. I refuse to fight. I would actually like to hear about your course.'

'Ectually?'

Alison stood up slowly and leaned on the table. 'Joan, I'm going to make some more coffee, and then, god dammit, can we talk about your course?'

Just like a hen, Joan thought, her solemn nod belied by the laughter brimming in her eyes. 'Yes, Ma'am!' she said earnestly, her voice just holding out. 'You must be one hell of a teacher.'

'You better believe it!' Alison came back smartly. She pointed a spoon accusingly at Joan. 'And I thought you were supposed to be one hell of a Local Government Officer?'

'Oh, I am, or was, and hope to god, I don't have to go back to being one.'

'You've quit your job?' Alison was shocked.

'Yes. And given up my flat.'

'It's that important?' Alison sat down again.

'I've burnt so many bridges this last month, it's a wonder you haven't noticed the glow in the sky to the north,' Joan said.

Feeling again her mother's hands on her shoulder, the worn wedding ring gleaming as those hands had tightened convulsively.

'Child, think! You boxing yourself into a corner. I always supported you. We, your father and I, we've always stood by you. But this! At least you have the sense to tell me first. It would kill him. Kill him, I tell you. He's so proud of you. Isn't it enough for you that you are black? Where you get this idea from? Women and women. That's white women's foolishness.'

Alison wanted to say something, mostly she wanted to touch Joan, but even the perspectives in the room seemed askew. Joan seemed light years away from her across the yellow formica. She bit her knuckle.

'Don't worry, you're not stuck with me. I've things to do in Birmingham, when I've finished.'

Alison ignored that. 'My god. You've got so much invested in this course,' she looked at Joan. 'I'd be terrified.'

Joan looked back at her. 'I am,' she said simply, and left the room.

Alison grabbed two handfuls of her own hair and hung on. Every instinct in her wanted to go after Joan. And do what? Say what? That those two quiet words had been like a depth-charge? That it wasn't fair? That she couldn't cope? That her exciting, dangerous, encounters with Joan had, up till now, been like being braced into a high wind on a cliff edge. But the wind had dropped with those two words. This was like those horrible falling dreams come back.

Joan walked back into the kitchen. Her eyes met Alison's warily. Alison slowly relaxed her drowning grip on her hair.

'Forgot the damned dishes!' Joan started to gather up her breakfast dishes. She paused halfway to the sink, and looked back over her shoulder. 'Bette Davis never has problems like this.'

Alison widened her eyes. 'Poor continuity, dahling!' she drawled. She gathered her own breakfast things and did her best Forties stalk towards Joan.

'Dahling!' Joan turned, 'where did you get that tee shirt?' One of her eyebrows lifted in disbelief, 'Not an ounce of padding in the shoulders!'

That broke them both up, but their laughter had a shaky, flinty edge. Alison risked a touch, her hand resting briefly, bravely, on Joan's arm. 'I'm sorry. Me and my significant insights!'

'Next time, knock before you walk into my mind, OK?' Joan turned away and began to wash the dishes. Wordlessly shaken, Alison picked up a towel and began to dry.

When Joan next spoke, her voice was gently conversational, her hands busy meticulously rinsing the sink and drainer. 'Is it OK to dance up here? I mean, what's the insulation like between the flats?'

'Pretty good, I think. They're purpose-built maisonettes. I only ever hear anything from downstairs if the windows are open.'

'Oh, at a pinch, I could use headphones. I just don't

want to bring down their chandeliers.'

'Are you likely to? What are you, a clog dancer?'

'You should see my half-Arkwright!' Joan said with an exaggerated Northern accent. 'In the classic North of Watford style of course.'

'Oh shit! Sorry!'

'Actually I was classically trained. Then I realised that none of the big ballet schools were going to snap me up.'

'Is that why you stopped dancing?'

'Who said I stopped?' Joan looked at Alison. What, she wondered, would you know about a fourteen-year-old's anger and mortification at not even being able to find ballet tights that were in her skin colour. The star pupil at the local dancing school, watching other, younger, white girls going on to the big academies.

'I switched to contemporary dance. It suited me, especially as I grew taller. I loved it.'

'Did you dance professionally?'

'Yes. Till I began to question the roles that I was being offered.'

'As a woman?'

'As a black woman.'

'I bet that's when things really got heavy.'

'Yeah. Then the very thing that gave me the most pleasure seemed to become a source of pain. And I don't use the world lightly. For a while I could barely walk, let alone dance.'

'What did you do?' Alison asked carefully, hardly daring to move.

'Had a disastrous affair with my physiotherapist.' Joan leaned back against the sink. 'You know the sort of thing, "Me Svengali – you whatever".'

'Trilby.'

'Yeah, Trilby.' Joan reached two cups down and Alison poured them both coffee. But they remained in the narrow galley area. Alison wanted a cigarette, but didn't dare move. Joan must have picked up the momentary shift of concentration and Alison felt her closing off.

'No, Joan. . . . please.'

Joan looked steadily at her for a moment. 'Do you want your cigarettes?'

'Please.'

Joan fetched them. From behind the business of lighting up Alison risked a question. 'What happened?'

'Oh, he began to feel he was losing ground to my politics. So he. . . .'

Alison did not hear the rest. He. All her assumptions were going out the window. Not all physiotherapists were female. Falling off the cliff time. Why did it hurt so much? The cup shook in her hand. She looked up into silence. Joan was miles off, unreachable.

Joan rinsed her cup. 'Must hit the books.' She moved towards the door, feeling that any dance she did now would probably explode the walls of the room.

'Joan!' Alison was compelled to speak. Joan paused in the doorway but did not turn. 'You do know that I'm a lesbian, don't you?'

Joan turned then. 'Yes. I've always known.'

They stared at each other. Alison looked down to stub out her cigarette, when she looked up again, Joan had gone.

'Oh shit!' Why, oh why, did it hurt so. Was that what Joan's shock was about at the meeting? Was that what was behind her reluctance to take up Alison's offer? Not because I'm white, but because I'm a lesbian? So many times, and each time it hurt like hell. To be drawn to someone, some woman, and then to see realisation dawn in their eyes. And read pity, distaste, amusement at her presumption, in the face before her. At least Joan never had to go through that. Not in the same way. What she was, was up-front, evident. She didn't have to go for days, weeks, wondering, doubting what someone's real feelings would be towards you, once they found out the true you. Hiding such a vital part of yourself. At work, because what you did was important, too important to risk. I'm a good teacher, Alison thought, the best science teacher they've had for years. And why? Because I care about the girls and young women that I'm teaching, because I don't need the power-trips. I can be fallible, share my excitement at new discoveries. And yet what would happen if they found out? No job, that's what would happen. Ridicule, scorn, hate. And Joan, what did Joan really feel about her? Alison didn't want to examine how she herself felt about Joan right now. Right now, she just wanted to get out of the flat. So much for her sanctuary against the world.

Joan closed the door carefully behind her, walked across to the window and stared unseeing out at the bare trees. So much for that, she thought. 'You do know that I'm a lesbian, don't you?' In other words, don't tell me about your nasty heterosexual past. If you don't have a sworn affidavit from your midwife, stating that you made a pass at her at birth, you're not a lesbian. The years of doubts, questioning, growing awareness, mean nothing. The fact that you're in love with the stupid woman means nothing. So much for my self-definition.

They saw each other at breakfast the next morning.

'Good luck with the course.'

'Thank you.'

'Shame we go in opposite directions, or I could have given you a lift.'

'I don't start till ten anyway.'

'Yes. I see. Bye!'

'Bye!'

That evening they met again, Alison grabbing a quick

snack on her way out to a meeting. Joan looked awful, strained and exhausted, but Alison didn't dare comment.

Joan thought that Alison was avoiding her and was quite relieved. She couldn't deal with anything else from Alison right now. Whatever she had expected from her course, it wasn't this. The group dance and movement sessions she could handle, just. And she was sure that after the first week, dancing with other people around would become easier, almost like being back in dance class. And there was the prospect of using one of the studios out of hours; space to really stretch herself again. She had worried most about the theoretical part of the course, unsure whether her part-time, extramural psychology courses would have given her enough background. Fully expecting to have to study hard most nights to keep up. She had been, justifiably she thought, quite proud of her dancing skills, and having to a certain extent reclaimed dance for herself, had wanted to use these skills to help other women. But here she was faced with the fact that the first woman that she would use dance therapy with would be herself. For, over the next ten weeks, working intensively with one of the tutors, she would have to analyse her own life and motivations. She did not yet know which of the tutors it would be, that would be decided at a meeting between herself and them at the end of the week. The prospect of this sort of self-analysis, while she was trying to cope with Alison, was not something that she was sure she could handle.

On Tuesday morning she stayed in her room till after Alison had left at eight thirty. When she came home that night Alison and another woman, Esther, were in the sitting room. Alison introduced them to each other, warily. Esther was faintly condescending, exceedingly curious, and took care, Joan thought, to establish her proprietory rights where Alison was concerned. Joan excused herself from joining them, and spent the evening in her room.

On Wednesday, they managed to avoid meeting each other completely.

Alison had been on her way home after a bad day at school. She had lost control of her last class, and the double period had deteriorated into a mess, with her barely able to function, and the girls taking advantage of this to rile her. And all day, growing from just a preoccupation, intensifying into a sensitised awareness to which her mind returned if not rigidly controlled, was the need to be with Joan. Becoming more urgent, more desperate as she drove home, till it seemed that she had no volition, but had to drive to the Centre.

'Joan Fisher. Hang on I'll see.' The man at the desk had said, and called to a woman on her way out. She had come over.

'You looking for Joan Fisher?'

'Yes, I'm her flatmate.'

'Ah. Yes.' Why had the woman looked at her like that? 'She's up in room four. She should be down soon.' And she'd left.

Alison waited for five minutes or so, the pulling towards Joan even more intense this close. She had no idea what she was going to say to her. Ostensibly they were estranged, barely speaking to each other, yet inside Alison there existed this, not so much a tugging, but an intense drawing towards the other woman, and an acute awareness that Joan shared this too. That the calling originated from her.

'Look, they're finished for the day. She won't be long. Why don't you go up. Number four is the small studio right at the end on the first floor.'

Alison went up the stairs and along the bare brick corridor of the converted warehouse until she came to room four. There was no window in the door, but there was the certainty of Joan's presence beyond it. The reasoning side of her mind was telling her how awful it was that she was here, intruding on something as important for Joan as this space. Suppose she was still with her tutor, in a seminar with a group of other people, and I turn up like an anxious mother hen? She'll decimate me. And yet, Joan had to be a part of this feeling, this needing. I'll just put my head quietly round the door, just to let her know that I'm here. She can ignore me if she's busy. Her hand seemed small and very white against the varnished wood of the door, and the force needed to move it seemed enormous. She saw only an empty segment of bare polished floor, so slid her body through the narrow opening.

Joan was dancing. In a big empty room with no barres or mirrors. Dancing by herself, but not alone, for her gestures and movements clearly outlined for Alison the partner, invisible, with whom she danced, or tried to dance. Again and again Joan would approach this other, trying to make her aware of her. Just the movement of her hand as she tenderly turned the invisible face towards her, only to have it turn heedlessly away, tightened Alison's throat, raised her off her heels, so that she felt herself beginning to flow forwards. Then Joan turned, naturally with the dance, and the shock of Alison's presence registered on her whole body. Shocking it into rigid immobility. As if she had crashed into a brick wall. And in Alison the shock reverberated, as if she too had crashed, jarring her back on her heels.

Joan's arm, outstretched in the dance, fell slowly to her side. Alison watched, unmoving, as the muscle tensions in the other woman's body altered to an enclosed watchful stillness. She became aware of the music at the same moment that Joan turned and crossed to a console in the corner. The music stopped, leaving a charged stillness that prickled on the skin of Alison's face. Joan turned back, and Alison wondered why she had not seized the chance to get out of there while her back had been turned. Except that it would not have got her very far. To the flat? A doubtful sanctuary, these days.

'Lost your keys? Lost your way?' Joan's voice was calm, yet Alison could feel the tension tightening. She was not aware of turning towards the door, but found herself looking at it over her shoulder when Joan's voice stilled her.

'No way, Alison!'

'Why not? *You* did on Sunday.'

'And I came back.'

'I don't mean the first time.'

'The second time, I didn't so much leave, as was shut out.'

'Just who is shutting who out?' From somewhere in her middle, Alison felt a small thread of anger uncoiling. 'That was a woman you were dancing with,' she accused.

'Just what is your problem with that, Alison? Aren't "born-again lesbians" allowed a fantasy life?' Joan was getting stiller and stiller, her eyes narrowed and dangerous.

'Problem?' Alison heard her voice rise. 'You could have told me on Sunday. But, no, you walked away and left me bleeding. Even after I felt compelled to come out to you. You just left me feeling . . .' her voice broke, 'feeling. . . .' She couldn't go on.

'Only after you made it quite plain that you didn't want to hear any more, Alison. Only after you shut down on me. It was hard enough for me to talk to you about things so important to me. There was no way that I was going to go on after you cut off.'

'I wasn't cutting off. It was just such a shock.'

'What was?' Joan was still not helping. 'The fact that I'd been with a man?'

No, thought Alison suddenly, the shock was that it

mattered so much to me. That it hurt so much. She was left speechless in the face of this realisation.

'You have no right to judge me, or my life, Alison.'

'And you had no right to keep something that important a secret from me. Especially after I told you about myself.'

'Which I already knew.'

'Exactly.'

'What do you mean, "exactly"? You have more than enough access to me already, Alison. How much more do you need? You already have more than anybody else, and you know it, or else you wouldn't be here.'

'And you're the first person that I ever asked to stay at my place.' Joan's head came up at that and she stared at Alison, some of the stillness leaving her.

'Not even Esther?'

Alison shook her head slowly. 'Over a long time ago.'

For you, but not for Esther, Joan thought, but did not speak aloud. Alison looked small and tired. Probably sleeping as badly as I am these last few days, Joan thought.

'For two women who can talk at each other the way we do, we don't communicate too well, do we?' Alison said.

'Not when we talk. But it seems we have other ways,' Joan said into the humming stillness of the room, some of the intent watchfulness leaving her eyes.

Alison walked towards Joan, stopping a few feet away. Slowly her arm lifted till her hand was held out. 'We were dancing, I believe?' she asked gently, bravely.

Joan said nothing for a moment, then she smiled rather wryly, and her hand came out to join Alison's. Alison placed her hand carefully in Joan's, and stepped off the cliff.

'We were,' Joan finally spoke, the admission surprisingly easy.

'We are,' Alison agreed firmly, not falling, but airborne.

'Yes,' Joan accepted, beginning the dance again, feeling her centre shift till it rested between them, with Alison's, in the strength of their clasped hands.

JUDY'S KISS

Michelene Wandor

You must know Judy. Everyone knows Judy.

Remember those early days of heady sisterhood? The groups of us, women, meeting, talking excitedly, sharing experiences, building sisterhood and solidarity, discovering that what was personal was political, that what we felt as our own little individual failings were really to do with social systems – with – well, I don't want this to turn into a tract, because it's a story. A fable, a parable, an allegory, a story about Judy. Judy the bright, Judy the beautiful, Judy the enthusiastic, Judy the creative, Judy whom we all loved and desired, who was everywhere and yet nowhere.

That's right. Everywhere and nowhere.

How can someone by everywhere and nowhere? Ubiquitous and absent, at one and the same time. Now you see her, now you don't. Clever, eh? Out of sleight, out of mind. On the high wire, through the flaming hoop, dare-devil acts of death-defying endeavour, and all in the gift of one woman. A heroine? No, not at all. The very opposite? We feminists don't believe in heroines, and therefore we don't believe in villains. We don't believe in saints and therefore we don't believe in devils. Or do we?

I'll start at the beginning. A group. A small group. A consciousness-raising group. A women's group. Judy arrives, a student, wearing jeans and a loose tee shirt (this is before the days of dungarees and kickers, remember), chain-smoking, bringing a bottle of cheap Spanish red plonk for her first meeting, just finished university, a degree in sociology clutched in her mind. There we were, a wonderfully motley collection, all feeling united, excited: Zelda, the pale poet, long dark hair hanging straight round her face, occasionally winged back behind her ears when she wanted to see out; Chrissie, mother of three, broad-hipped, swaying in her long skirts as she walked, warm and angry; Anna, slight, wearing jeans and plimsolls with flowers drawn on them with Pentels, short, short hair, quiet and watchful; Susan, loud, dynamic actress, left the Royal Shakespeare Company to do political theatre; and me – well it's always hard to describe yourself with what you feel is real objectivity; after all, I'm not new to myself in the way the others were new to me. So I won't say much about me, except that I don't talk an awful lot. (Susan used to get very paranoid about my silences, she used to say she felt I disapproved of her somehow – but that's another story.) But I do listen and watch, and all through those years I kept a careful diary of some of the things we talked about.

We met as a regular weekly group for about five years. I don't think I'll ever experience anything quite like it again; and it isn't something you can describe easily to other people. After the meetings my head would be buzzing with thoughts, ideas, disagreements – anyway, I'm straying off the point again. This story is really a compilation of a pattern of events which were slowly woven over a period of years – the years after the group stopped meeting. We stopped meeting as a group because people began to drift off into other lives and activities. But we had established a real specialness, we had lived through years of self- and political discovery which would never be forgotten.

And especially never forgotten because of Judy. Judy left the group first. My diary doesn't say much about the events that led up to her leaving. But it does note the week she dashed in (cigarette smoking, and the usual bottle of wine) entirely clothed in orange. She had seen the light, she had found new belief, she was going to India to follow a guru. We were, of course, dumbfounded; we argued, we wept, we raged — but she was sweetness and light, told us we didn't understand, that you could only know what it felt like by experiencing it, that she loved us all very, very much, and that she was flying to India at the weekend, this would be her last meeting, should she open her bottle of wine now? And of course we all loved one another by then, and we all believed in the right to self-determination for women, and none of us really dared to utter the feelings of loss, betrayal, bewilderment which we all felt deep down as individuals, so we drank the wine; Chrissie, whose house we met in, brought in some cinnamon toast, and then Judy went round and kissed each of us goodbye. I can't speak for the kisses the others got, but my kiss was soft and light and moist and full on the lips and fleeting and gentle. And then Judy whirled away early because she had to pack and talk over arrangements with the group she was travelling with.

Now I'm sure that Judy was not responsible for breaking up the group; but the facts are that soon after her departure we began meeting less often, and after about a year of desultory meetings we sort of stopped meeting. As I said before, people were drifting off into other busy-nesses, or leaving London for short or long periods, so it felt natural. It felt like growing up. And of course, after so much time we were always in each other's minds and hearts. We ran into each other in ones or twos or more, in different permutations, exchanged gossip, concern, kept up with each other's lives. We found also that whenever any of us met, the conversation, within a very short space of time turned to Judy. Where was she, what was she doing, who had heard from her — perfectly ordinary questions, but always tinged with an edge, an expectation, an urgency – a something never quite voiced.

The years passed. And some six or seven years later, telephone lines were buzzing. We had each received a gilt-embossed card announcing Judy's marriage. To someone we'd never heard of. Were we all going? What did we all think? Anyway, after filling British Telecom's coffers for some weeks, we all decided to go. And I had a little brainwave. What do you think, I asked everyone, if we have a group get-together, a sort of reunion for all of us, just before the wedding? A sort of hen-party, but of a different sort. The first time for years, the six of us in the same room. I would cook, it could be at my place. No, no, don't bring anything. It will be my pleasure.

On the appointed evening we all gathered. It wasn't like a reunion of people who had been estranged for ages – but it was the first time we had all occupied the same space, and it was like the old times. We were at ease, we were eager, excited we all talked nineteen to the dozen. We drank some wine – and after about an hour I wondered whether we should start without Judy – for she was the only one who hadn't turned up. We then all wondered out loud where she was – I rang the phone number where I thought she was staying, but there was no reply. We tried another few contacts, but no one knew where she was. So we hung on for another few moments, and then we decided to eat.

After a delicious meal (if I do say so myself) we settled to coffee, and then, just like that, out of the blue, I heard myself say: 'OK, what about Judy, then?'

They all looked a bit puzzled. 'What do you mean?' asked Anna.

'Judy,' I said. 'We've been eating and talking about everything under the sun except what's obsessing us most. Judy.'

'Don't know what you're talking about,' said Susan.

But she did, and she was grinning to prove it.

'Look,' I said, 'Judy's not here, but we're all thinking about her, aren't we? We always talk about her to each other, and yet tonight we haven't mentioned her. Why?'

'It would feel a bit like gossiping,' offered Anna.

'That depends on how we talk about her,' said Chrissie. 'Anyway, what's wrong with gossip? We do it all the time.'

'Right,' I said – perhaps feeling confidence because it was my territory, my flat. 'Let's just do the traditional thing, chat about Judy, and then get back to other things.'

There was a little silence. 'She isn't here – she hasn't let us know – we don't know where she is – ' I was floundering a bit, not quite sure how to put my suggestion into practice.

'Perhaps she doesn't exist,' said Anna softly.

Some of us laughed, some of us were silent. 'Of course she exists,' said Zelda.

'All right,' said Anna. 'Tell us about her.'

There was another little silence. I jumped up to make another large pot of coffee, and when I'd got back, done all the pouring and we were newly settled, Zelda took up the gauntlet.

'After Judy came back from India, after she'd given up the guru, I ran into her in a pub one evening. I was reading my poetry – along with some other poets, a comedy act, and then a band at the end of the evening – you know the sort of thing. Well, it doesn't matter if you don't. Anyway, it was great seeing Judy, and she said she really enjoyed hearing my poetry, and she'd started writing poetry as well, and could she send me some, and she was all shy – well, it was great to see her. She was all over the orange stuff, she said, and wanted to be a real writer now. She sent me some poetry and came round – and it was good, actually, quite different from mine, and I sent her some poems I'd been working on, and then she sent me some of hers, and we sort of went on like that. Then it got a bit weird. She started sending me some poems that I thought somehow imitated mine. I know that sounds paranoid – I can't quite explain it. I just felt she was doing it. But of course I didn't say anything, because it was so silly.

'Then at one reading I did, I suggested that she should read some of hers as well. She was a bit scared, but she came – and our stuff went really well together, and we had a really good evening, got pissed; it was great. I felt really inspired – you know how sometimes you do, and I suggested trying to set up some more readings where we worked out a bit of a programme together. Judy was really keen, and then at the end of the evening we both rushed off, all keen, and she gave me a nice, soft, moist kiss goodnight on the cheek.

'I chased around one or two places, and managed to fix up two joint readings. I rang her up to tell her and she was in this terrible rush; she couldn't make either of the dates because she was reading with some new group of young poets. And then after that I started seeing her name with this group, doing readings all over the place.'

'Didn't you say anything to her?' asked Anna.

'What could I say?' said Zelda. 'I mean, I thought about it. But then I thought she had a perfect right to do what she wanted, I had no claim on her, did I.'

'But didn't you feel she'd let you down?' Anna went on.

'Of course. Especially when I heard that she was the one who had got the other group together and she hadn't included me. I just left it. It seemed – petty somehow. To mention it, I mean.'

Chrissie took up the baton next: 'Maybe this is trivial as well. Remember when I was pregnant with Jacob – ' We all nodded. Chrissie had become pregnant with her fourth child just as the group was winding down, and she was just getting into all kinds of weird and exciting ways of giving birth – to music in a darkened room – strange stuff – but she went on: 'Well, Judy got in touch with me about a month before he was born. She'd heard that I was pregnant, she'd heard I wanted to do it my way and she was really pleased for me, it sounded so *autonomous* and natural. At the time I was completely self-absorbed, and she was just marvellous. She kept dropping in to visit me, put her hand on my stomach to feel Jacob kick, read all my books, and we talked endlessly about what sort of music I wanted. She wanted to be there with me, she said, it would be so marvellous, such sisterhood, such a sharing experience. Her timing was amazing. She rang up the week Barry pissed off.' (Barry was Chrissie's then husband.)

'It wasn't just that I wanted a substitute for Barry – but it was the thought that there would be another woman there with me as well. Judy talked a lot about primitive ritual and motherhood, and we made lists of names and everything.

'Anyway, the week before Jacob was due, Judy dropped round with a book about childbirth in the Third World, and literally at the door, after she'd kissed me goodbye, a soft, moist kiss on the cheek, she said she'd give me a ring when she got back. She was going to China with a woman she'd fallen in love with. I didn't know that at the time. But she sent me a postcard from China, and it was clear from that.'

'Oh dear,' said Anna.

'But just like Zelda, I didn't say anything to her, either at the time or afterwards. I don't know why. Perhaps I felt too let down to dare say anything.'

'But you must have felt terrible,' said Anna.

'Oh, I wanted to kill her,' said Chrissie, very calmly. 'Most unsisterly, wasn't it? I think I knew that I would either kill her, or say nothing at all. And since I didn't want to be had up for murder, I kept quiet.'

'Oh, dear,' said Anna again.

'I got over it,' said Chrissie. 'It doesn't bother me now at all. That's why I can talk about it for the first time.'

'I meant oh dear for a different reason,' said Anna. 'The woman Judy went to China with was me.'

To a woman our heads whipped round in total amazement. Chrissie burst out laughing, and we all relaxed, while Anna still looked worried – 'Look, Chrissie, I'm really sorry – ' Chrissie was laughing so much she couldn't speak, she just waved her hand in front of her as if to say 'Don't be sorry' – then her laughter turned into a minor coughing fit, and by the time I'd got a glass of water, and she'd been patted on the back, the air was clearer again, though Anna still looked a little tense.

'What happened was that Judy came to stay in my house. Well, the North London commune I was living in at the time.'

We all groaned a bit, in memory of the way we'd sent up poor old Anna for being so earnest about collective living all those years ago.

'Anyway,' said Anna, 'it seemed revolutionary at the time – I'm not going to let you lot turn me cynical. Judy and I were lovers. We were having a relationship while she was visiting you, Chrissie, I suppose. She never said anything to me about the baby – I didn't drag her to China to stop her being with you, honestly – '

'Really, Anna, it doesn't matter. I'm not blaming you. Finish your story about Judy.' Chrissie was once more calm and reassuring.

'All right,' said Anna. 'We were crazy about each other. We worked in a food co-op, we held hands when we went shopping in the market, we wore Lesbians Unite badges, we went on demos, we went to women-only discos, we made paintings on cardboard with our menstrual blood and then hung them on the wall of our bedroom. We made love on my huge mattress on the floor and we told each other our dreams and cooked lentil stews, and then one day we decided to move out of the commune together and live in a flat, just the two of us. We found a flat, we bought pots and pans and painted the wall in bright colours and we moved in, and then one night Judy got up with a bad headache, she said, and I went back to sleep, and the next morning she wasn't in bed. She'd sat up all night in the kitchen, and I was really worried about her, but she flung her arms round me, and her eyes were all shining and she said she'd decided that her vocation in life was to be a writer, and she gave me a soft, moist kiss on the mouth, and she spent the rest of the day crying and packing and saying she would never forget me, I was the most important person in her life, she would still love me and we would still make love but she needed some solitude, a place on her own, a room of her own and I must understand.

'Then she went. We never made love again after that. There was always some perfectly good reason. Never the "I've got a headache" though.'

We all laughed, though I'm not sure if we were all laughing at the same thing. But it didn't matter.

'Where did she go?' asked Chrissie.

'She wouldn't tell me,' said Anna. 'She said it was a little room, and she wanted it to be her own, private, it had to be that way. So I respected it.'

'Did you ever find out?' asked Chrissie.

'Yes,' said Anna. 'I overheard someone in a bookshop talking about going to supper with her and her boyfriend at an address somewhere in Battersea.'

'Well, I never,' said Susan, who had been unusually quiet all this time.

'I didn't say anything about it to her,' said Anna. 'If she felt she had to lie to me, then there wasn't anything I could do about it. Or perhaps I didn't want to re-open the whole painful business. I don't know.'

'I'll give you the address, if you like,' said Susan. We all looked a bit puzzled.

'The address Judy moved to.'

I started laughing. Susan joined in.

'My house in Battersea. Well, our house in Battersea. Well, the house that Pete's father had given us the down-payment for, and which we'd also had a go at turning into a kind of collective house.'

Susan had all our attention. She went on: 'The house really worked well as a collective thing, as long as Pete and I were OK. And we were fine for ages. We had occasional other relationships, but we both knew about them, and it seemed to work out for quite a long time. Judy turned up one day in a taxi with nowhere to stay, and we had a room free. Simple as that. By coincidence, well, I think it was coincidence, Pete and I started bickering quite a lot – I don't know why. I was really pleased to see Judy, she was always so sympathetic. I'm afraid I spent hours in the kitchen talking to her about the house, Pete and me – oh, I was really grateful to her. Then one day I got home early from work, went to make a cup of tea, and there in the kitchen was Judy, listening in exactly the same way to Pete. There was something about the way they were both sitting, at opposite ends of the table – I just knew they'd been having more than just a conversational relationship. There was a sort of electricity about it all. Pete and I had always had an agreement that we would never have sexual relationships with other people who were actually living in the house. Of course no one said anything, I never accused anyone, after all, we're all free agents, aren't we – anyway. I decided to move out. The day I was moving, Judy invited a whole lot of people over to lunch, just as if nothing had happened. And there was I, dragging my cases downstairs, Pete and me both upset, and all these total strangers flooding into the house to have a good boozy time. I haven't seen Judy since.'

No one asked Susan why she hadn't said or done anything. Everyone turned to me.

'You remember all those long stories I used to tell about my theatre company – well, it wasn't actually mine, the one I worked in as administrator. Well, a few years after Judy came back from India she got in touch with me, said she was keen to get some kind of work, any old dogsbody job, she didn't mind, just as long as it was something to do with the group. So she filled in occasionally in the office, doing odd bits of typing, now and again coming on tour with us, loading the van, driving sometimes, very easy-going, very jolly. Then we began to have all sorts of splits and differences in the company – Judy wasn't involved in any of the arguments directly, because she wasn't really a member of the company. And partly because I thought of her as my friend, I used to let off steam to her, talk about it, complain about people I thought were a pain – you know the sort of thing.

'Judy was a good listener, and she nodded a lot, and I felt she was sympathetic and with me. Then there was a sort of secret coup, where a handful of people planned to leave and start a breakaway company with the same name. It was all very murky, and they fiddled money and heaven knows what else – and we were arguing about the name, and who had the right to the offices and everything, and in the middle of all this I got a letter from Judy saying she'd been asked to join the other company as its administrator. I didn't quite know what to do about this. Was she asking my permission, my approval? I was trying to work out what to do, when quite by chance when I was in the office one day, I found the proof of a poster for the breakaway company's first show, and Judy's name was down there as administrator. So of course I realised that she had taken the job long before she wrote me the letter. So I did nothing.

'That wasn't the end of it, though. There were still a lot of things to sort out; the breakaway group got up a lobby to the Arts Council to prove that they were the 'real' group, and should get a grant, and it was spear-headed by Judy, who wrote press releases, statements to the press, and became a sort of minor celebrity for a while. The weird thing was that the way she wrote, the way she presented the arguments were all the things I'd said, but turned round to apply to the other group. She was using all my arguments.

'As you know, our group fell apart – exhaustion, partly I think, and I left to go back to teaching. But that year I got a Christmas card from Judy, with a hasty scrawl saying she was terribly busy, and she knew that although we'd been briefly professional rivals, we would always be good friends. The card had a kiss on it, in red Pentel, but sort of smudged, as though something wet had blurred it.'

We were all silent. We shifted a little in our chairs. We looked at our hands, at each other. We wondered where to go next, what to do with these stories, these bits of each other's lives of which we'd been unaware, these stories about ourselves and Judy.

'There were some nice things – ' I offered, half statement, half question. We came up with a list of things in a rush: appropriate birthday presents, get-well cards, invitations to supper, a phone call during a depression. But somehow we tipped back into other things – offhand exchanges which had stuck and were not yet exorcised – and somehow none of us quite knew what we were really saying about Judy. Was she a friend or wasn't she? Was she nice or was she nasty? Were we all cowards, or generous and tolerant, or mean and nasty? Chrissie said something about the ethics of personal behaviour, and we all jumped on that, saying it wasn't just the ethics, it was how we all felt. Anyway, it was all a great jumble – just like old times, I thought – and then there didn't seem much more to say.

'Well,' said Anna, 'I suppose if this was some sort of formal inquiry we would want to see if there was more evidence against the accused.'

'Come on,' said Chrissie, 'she's not on trial. Anyway, if she was, it would only be right to let her defend herself.'

But we all agreed that we didn't want to do anything like that. There was another silence.

'Well,' said Susan, 'what are we going to do, then?'

'Nothing, I suppose,' I said. 'Just like we always have.'

'No. We've got to make a decision,' said Susan.

'What about?' asked Zelda.

'What we're each going to wear for the wedding,' said Susan.

We fell about. Of course. We all simply had to go to the wedding. We all simply had to see whether Judy looked different to us all, now that we had shared all these bits of unfinished business with one another. We launched onto a wonderful and extensive discussion about what we should wear to the wedding. glitter or wool? black or fluorescent pink? high heels, pumps? trousers, long skirt? We each talked our way through our wardrobes, and then decided that whatever we each chose, we must all also wear something old, something new, something borrowed and something blue. I then made a final pot of peppermint tea, to calm down our wonderfully stimulated brains, and as we sipped, preparatory to saying goodbye, Susan said in a casual and offhand tone: 'By the way, have you noticed where the wedding reception is being held?' We checked our invitations, and there was an address in Battersea, which, now we looked at it, was really rather familiar.

'That's it,' said Susan. 'That's the house Pete and I lived in, where Judy came to stay.'

'But how –,' I started.

'Well, it's quite logical,' said Susan. 'After I left, Judy moved out the next day. Pete stayed, because it was his money that was really in the house. Everyone else left, and Pete now lives there alone. Judy rang him up and asked him if she could borrow the house for the reception because she had had such happy times there. It's quite logical, when you think about it. Utterly tactless, but entirely logical.'

'If I'd known, I'd have invited Pete over this evening,' I said. Susan grinned.

The evening broke up in utterly scurrilous jollity.

Now that could be the end of the story – and in a way it is the end of the story proper. But there is an important postscript to this story, which possibly makes it into an improper story. I don't know. See what you think.

On the appointed day we went to the registry office. Judy was wearing dazzling white, mid-calf-length lace, with a transparent net piece over her neck, shoulders and the tops of her breasts. She did look lovely. We stood through the brief and functional ceremony and I must admit I had some rather naughty thoughts shooting through my mind. Ah, I thought, here we have another category to add to our collection: to Judy the Poet, Judy the Mystic, Judy the Lesbian, Judy the Heterosexual, Judy the Feminist, Judy the Confidante – we can now add Judy the Virgin. I stored the thought up for future possible use.

At the reception we stood in a well-groomed group: Anna, Zelda, Chrissie, Susan and me, watching Judy do the rounds of all the guests whose stories we did not know. On a table in the middle of the room stood a splendid wedding cake, and at the appropriate moment Judy and her groom went across to be photographed cutting the cake. The hubbub of conversation in the room quietened and people turned towards the focal centre. Just as the photographer was getting his camera set up, we all saw Judy looking up at her groom, who made some remark to her. She laughed in reply, and reached up on tiptoe to kiss his cheek, a soft, moist, slightly lingering kiss.

And then it happened. Judy disappeared. We all saw it – that is, Anna, Zelda, Chrissie, Susan and me. On the groom's cheek was the soft glisten of a moist kiss, but of Judy all there was was the white dress, pure and empty. We saw it. We looked at one another. But none of us said anything, because no one else had noticed anything out of the ordinary.

They were all looking at their own Judy, their own incomplete, unfinished Judy. They all carried the memory of that single, moist kiss. But not us. We knew now for sure that she did not exist. And so incredibly full of collective relief were we, that we knew that never again would we have to tell each other a single story about her. Never again.

The wedding cake was absolutely delicious.

A FINE ROMANCE

Ann Oosthuizen

'When I phoned Jean,' Milly looked slyly at me to see when I got the joke, 'she was talking with her mouth full.' She imitated the voice: 'Hang on . . . er . . . I'm just eating a mars bar out of . . . well, actually . . . Mary. You can speak to her if you like.'

We giggled.

'Was Mary *able* to say anything?' I asked.

'Not a lot. She used to be a rampant heterosexual until she met Jean. Well, Jean is just too much – amazing.'

When I was with Milly it was hard to believe we were running a business. It was hard anyway. We worked in a tiny office furnished with a second-hand carpet and two desks rescued from a skip. When I invoiced mail-order parcels of books, I had to convince myself that I wasn't still playing shop with pretend money and empty cartons of cornflakes. As the work was part-time, we hardly ever saw each other, but when we did we always shared a picnic lunch on the carpet, played Capital Radio and talked about sex – mostly about how we didn't get it – and we encouraged each other's elaborate stratagems to ensnare the men we had our eyes on.

Being the only two heterosexuals on the collective made us light-headed when we were on our own, so the idea of a whole day together, paid to be out of the office, seemed like a holiday, although we were actually on our way to an important meeting. We had an appointment with a buyer for the biggest distributor in the country.

'We should show Hugh Grant next year's titles,' I'd urged. 'We'll never get a chance like this again – if he took the two novels, we could sell thousands.'

'I'd discovered Hugh Grant by accident when he was at W. H. Smith's. He was sympathetic in a way which made it clear he'd like to give us a push in the right direction. His wife was a feminist, he said, and I'd heard from another publisher that he'd been a socialist at Oxford. Whatever the reason, he seemed susceptible to pressure from our uncompromising feminist co-operative.

'If we can get in there,' I'd enthused, 'we're made. Every woman in Britain will be seeing our books. These people actually choose the top ten best sellers and then supply all the newsagents, and it all starts in Godalming. Do you know which station we leave from?'

'It's commuter belt – must be Waterloo.'

It could have been on the moon.

We'd both dressed up. Milly was in her Lou Reed outfit: black hat and blazer with narrow black trousers. The scarf at her neck was black chiffon with gold glitter. I was in my dress. I hate winter because then I have to wear the shapeless rabbit fur I bought cheap in Oxford Street years ago. It's the only thing that keeps me warm, but it doesn't make me look successful. Perhaps I could slip it off the moment we were inside the building.

Milly waves her hands around a lot, so her skinny black arms punctuated her speech in semaphore. We were so absorbed in our talk that we almost forgot to get off at the station, exploding onto a platform that was as deserted as a Sunday afternoon.

'Where's everybody? There's no taxis,' I wailed.

'It's early. Let's go into town first – I'm starving.'

The town, as always two blocks downhill from the station, looked as if it was made from a kit marked Affluent Southern UK. There were small branches of

Marks and Spencer, Miss Selfridge and Debenhams in a narrow, curving main road jam-packed with sparkling small cars all with recent registration numbers. Rejecting Ben's Diner, we settled for what looked like an inexpensive tudor snack bar. It was only when we had sat down at the empty table in the window and ordered our egg and chips that we realised what we had let ourselves in for.

None of the usual chatter and busy feeling of lunchtime rush. In the silence you could hear a crumb drop.

'What's going on here?' I asked Milly in what was meant to be *sotto voce*, but sounded like a bellow.

She jumped, and gave me an imperious frown.

I turned my head. The whole room was spread out in front of me. There were about half a dozen tables and at each one sat a woman on her own. They were all tidily dressed, their hair curled, their coats hung neatly on the rack near the door. One toyed with a tea cup, another cut a cheese sandwich into smaller sections and placed a piece delicately in her mouth.

'It's depressing . . . ' I started.

'Please don't go on about it. Let's get out of here.' Milly was shovelling tomato sauce over her chips.

An old lady in the corner who had ordered tea, counted out her sixteen pence carefully onto the table cloth. She was joined by a thick-set woman in a cream raincoat.

'I've paid for my tea,' she quavered.

'That's nice, dear,' the other one replied, putting her large brown bag onto an empty chair and settling back with a sigh.

A woman in her forties sat miserably over a salad lunch, picking at a lettuce leaf. At the table next to her two grey-haired matrons, wearing identical navy felt hats and beige constumes, weren't saying a word.

'Excuse me . . . ' Milly tried to order tea.

'Just a minute. I'll be with you as soon as I can.' The waitress was serving coffee at the back. She was formidable in her red suit, resolutely determined to keep us in our place.

The women stared in an unfocused way towards the centre of the room. They didn't want to catch my eye – or anyone else's.

'Hurry up,' urged Milly. 'This place gives me the wobblers. Stop looking at everyone – they'll get mad at us.'

'I have to,' I whispered back. 'Can't you see – they're my age, or close. They could be me.'

'Go on.'

I forgot to mention that I am twenty-five years older than Milly. I'm also nearly a foot shorter. Outside on the pavement, I took little runs to keep up with her.

'Don't you see?' I gasped. 'They're in a state of profound depression. Wouldn't you be?'

Milly didn't want to talk about it, but I was determined.

'We need to break through that terrible loneliness. They probably think it's just them who can't cope.'

At this point I have to declare myself. I had expected to sell thousands of copies of our first book within weeks of publication. I had imagined van loads being delivered to bookshops where grateful owners would rush to place them in their shop windows while women queued for each title, passing copies from hand to hand so that they became dog-eared with concentrated passion.

I hadn't been prepared for shop-keepers who said they didn't think anyone would want to buy, or who placed the book out of sight, gathering dust, where women couldn't even find out about it. We sold enough to keep us afloat, but not a flood – and we still weren't getting to the unconverted.

Would we ever? It was like a huge stone we needed to roll.

'Those ghostly presences in the cafe – they're on the scrap heap all right and they know it. They've every reason to feel depressed – I'm depressed every time I look in the mirror. It takes all my effort of will to pretend I feel OK about my wrinkles. Of course I don't.'

Milly's a good friend. She always knows when the rhetoric has hit a rock. 'You're beautiful,' she said. 'I wouldn't want you any younger.'

'Really?' I started to feel more cheerful. I stole a glance at her fashionably thin young body. 'Do you think you're the closest thing to a punk this town has ever seen?' I was proud to be with her.

This time we found a taxi at the station which carried us off to a collection of single-storied brick buildings on an industrial estate. The receptionist sat behind a counter in a small glass hallway which looked as if it had been put up five minutes before our arrival.

'Your appointment with Mr Grant?' she said cheerfully. 'Oh yes, he's busy just at the moment. He asks you please to take a seat.'

We must look respectable enough, I thought with relief. In the toilet I took off my coat and fluffed up my hair. I needed a haircut. Well, I'd have to rely on Milly to impress him with her looks. Back in the waiting area Milly was already studying the advanced information sheets and publicity schedules she had prepared. I walked over to the large rubber plant standing in the corner and rehearsed my arguments. Both of us were edgy and excited. The books that get marketed from there don't depend on reviews for sales – their choice is made in that unimpressive building before the public has even heard of them.

After he had rung through to the receptionist Hugh Grant met us in the corridor outside his room and shook us both warmly by the hand. He was a large, fair-skinned man with a disarming lisp. Ordering coffee from a woman surrounded by cartons of books, he showed us to seats at a mahogany table pushed up against the wall of his office. We were getting the full treatment! I manoevred Milly between him and myself. Behind him was a rack of the best sellers for the year, placed so that the front covers were all displayed. These were the books I had dreamed of emulating.

'We believe that the book trade, particularly the popular market, has ignored the phenomenal growth in the demand for feminist books.'

He nodded.

'I understand that women make up 80 per cent of your customers, and they now do want to read feminist books. You can see that by the way feminist presses have flourished, especially at a time when most publishers have experienced recession rather than growth.' I was pleased with myself – I sounded convincing.

'Let me explain,' he said carefully, 'how we choose our titles.'

'Please. It would be a great help to us.'

'We choose ten titles each month, which we will push through all our bwanches. We look at covers four months in advance of publication, and make our choice partly on that. I'd be happy to advise you if you want to send me wough dwafts. We find pastel shades sell well.'

The boudoir colours on the books winked at me. Women, mostly in period costume, stood framed by purple landscapes fading into pink skies. Not photographs, but idealised drawings represented the characters in each novel. A man buried his rugged profile in the arched neck of a dark-eyed beauty. Her eyes were fixed on a grove of palm trees in the distance, her auburn curls tumbled over her shoulders. We could do something like that, I thought. If the collective agrees. Well, not exactly like that, but sort of.

It was Milly's cue. She was showing him the publicity material. He was reading through it thoroughly.

'Yes, we'd be intewested, especially in the thwiller.

Family sagas are doing well too at the moment.'

'Does it have to retail at a very low price?' I was apprehensive on this point.

'Not any more. It can go as high as £2.50.'

Again I thought, well, we can do that. If they take it we could do a bigger print run. Bring down the price.

'The main thing is,' he went on, 'we back well-known authors.'

I'd seen that. I ticked the names off. It seemed as if the same few writers supplied the whole market.

'But we will look at a new author. It depends on the size of the advertising budget, and where it is placed. We look to see how far publishers are pwepared to back their choice.'

'How much would you expect us to spend?'

'For a new novel – awound £15,000.'

That was almost half our yearly turnover! The purple and mauve books framed his head like a comforting, soft duvet. We didn't have enough money to get into the market, even in disguise. I had to try harder.

'But you're only pushing established escape literature – romantic pulp.'

'People wead to escape – '

'Oh, I know. I've heard that women say reading romances is like having a different man every night . . . '

He blushed, and ducked his head as if avoiding a troublesome insect.

I was too disappointed to stop. 'You sell books as if they were soap. . . . Books are . . .'

He smiled in a tired way. He had decided to sit this one out.

'Oh – you already know the arguments – '

Milly kicked me. I don't remember the conversation after that. It was about trade terms, discounts, minimum orders. I wrote down what he said, but my heart wasn't in it.

We didn't talk much on the way back. I was in a gloomy mood as the train sped past all those houses with their pretty back yards.

'They'll never let us in. They'll make sure the world can never change. It's a conspiracy.'

Milly wasn't going to be drawn so easily. I had to go deeper.

'You know, the most ridiculous thing is that I *know* all those books – I could recite every word; it's the same rubbish I used to devour as a child. I bet if you opened me up, you'd find I was still Cinderella inside.'

'Me too. I read the mags in the doctor's waiting room like a secret vice.'

'An addiction?'

'Yes *and* I cry at the happy endings.'

We fell about laughing at the madness of it.

'Lucky it doesn't happen to us! 'I gasped.

Milly opened her arms to the carriage roof. 'We're saved from a fate worse than death – True Love.'

'Hold me tight,' I begged her. 'Tell me I'm real.'

She did. 'You're real all right. You were spectacular today.'

'WHO'S SHE –
THE CAT'S MOTHER?'

Marsha Rowe

It is the corner of Kylie's room a Greek visitor admired
once seeing the white curve of the chimney breast, the
narrow bench next to it, the stained floorboards. 'So like
Greece,' the visitor exclaimed softly, astonished, stroking
the alabaster wall, 'and not like England at all.'

Kylie laughed. 'I bought this there,' she admitted,
meaning the Greek, rough seersucker sheet, also white,
tucked over the cushion along the bench. Quite high, the
bench built against the wall.

Tonight Kylie sits quite high and straight on it,
watching Janet. On the old, low, dark table between them
there are tea things on a tray. Then there is Janet on the
ticking-striped couch. Janet is wearing something blueish
– later Kylie can never remember what because she saw
Janet afterwards always wearing bronzes and plum
reddish-browns which made her eyes look paler and
greener – whereas tonight they are an adjudicating blue,
reflective in an enigmatic, contained sort of way but not
cunning, gentle when she casts over at Kylie occasional,
cool looks. And she is sitting on the couch because she is
clearly that sort of visitor. Rather neat with a cat's
absolute claim on comfort and location. Yet her thick,
combed-out fair-brown hair is standy-out and wilder so
she does not look prim at all. Possibly she was reluctant
to come today. She was late.

'You want to live in Leeds?'

Janet nods, her job in Manchester merely the first step to moving out of London.

'It's such a long way to go to work from here every day.'

'No-o.' Janet's reply is singularly final because Kylie doesn't catch her faint Scottish accent.

Everything has been said about rent, housework rotas, about how the house is merely a collective, just about viable, that no special friendship amongst them is expected.

About all that Kylie is relieved, leaning back against the chalk white wall on her high, white bench surveying her visitor, relieved and a little bewildered.

Her own eyes are dark, brown-black, lively and intense dark. Her belly is occupied and rising. Her brown-black hair is losing its curl, just as her mother said it would, one of those commonplace mysterious things of pregnancy. To Janet the belly, the dark eyes, dark hair, are all a bit voluptuous and darkish, especially amidst the arty, virginal white room and all the black-and-white-striped stuff, the couch, Kylie's dungarees, even the rug on the polished boards.

In this pale, stripey, spacey atmosphere Kylie and Janet recognise something about each other which is making them both curious and a little wary. They leave each other cold, the two women, but there is something. So that Janet is not coming right out with it, not saying immediately that she will move into the house with Kylie, but they both think she will quite likely and they are both breathing a little easier.

'Neil always said it was a collection of bedsits,' Kylie says with a laugh, leaning even farther and higher back against the white wall. The space between the two women is more than they bargained for. Absolutely no rapport nor arrangements-of-guilt. No promises. So far, so good. 'Neil used to have the room next door. That's going to be the baby's room. Why don't we go downstairs then you can look at the room you might have?' Janet has already asked a lot of questions about her weaving, about Leeds, and she is tired. She's been working all day and there is more to do this evening.

Downstairs they go. Graceful, wide Victorian stairs made for descents in wide skirts Kylie often thinks, and maids' passing, but now covered in Bill's aunt's cast-off carpet, until they reach the stained glass door to the back room. Its musty gold, green and pink diamonds nippled in crimson always remind Kylie uncomfortably of a church. 'It's quite a cold room,' Kylie warns as she opens the door, 'those two outside walls need insulating. But there is the central heating and the gas fire.'

Janet likes the high, narrow room and its curved bay of three high windows each with a top sash of more stained-glass. She catches sight of herself in one of the old mirrors set into the wall between them. Her brown-blonde hair looks more platinum. Quite flattering. Cold! She grew up in Edinburgh.

'Bill will be back on Saturday. You could meet him then. And it was Sol who told you we were looking for someone. So that's all of us. And you've got a bed and stuff? If you decide you want to move in?'

'Oh, yes. Aah. And two cats.' Janet looks out the window and considers. The cats.

'Oh. Do you?'

'They're a scatty pair. I, er,' Janet stops. What a wild back garden. Must be a hundred feet. Privet rampant against the light, evening sky. Towering thistles. Butter-cups. Just below, blackberries wind over gooseberries in a barbed, choked tangle.

'We used to grow lots of vegetables. And strawberries. Now only Bill does any gardening and this summer he's only had time to plant some spinach and some lettuce. You can't see them from here, can you?' Kylie looks out beside Janet. 'The lettuce is wonderful. Unusual. Salad Bowl, it's called. Its leaves are all frilly and tuckered.'

At the end of the weed-dotted drive, beyond the iron gates, three large dogs are yelping and chasing each other in circles. They run off down the lane. There's a pear tree and a tall, narrow building in red Leeds brick.

'That's called the giraffe house. It used to be the coach house. Underneath the kitchen there's the old stable.' Is Janet interested? More quiet. More space. 'I have a cat too. Called Vasya. What are yours?'

'I've never given mine names. There's a black and white one like Sylvester in the cartoon. He's the demanding one,' Janet claws in the air and miaows, laughs, turns back to face the room, 'and a female. She's all black and rather retiring.'

Kylie, suddenly light-headed, walks towards the gas fire. 'There used to be a mantelpiece over here but the others voted to take it down so the room would look wider. A pity. It's still down in the stable. Um. Bill doesn't approve of pets. Sol likes them but he's hardly ever here. Anyway, I've got Vasya. And Bill will just have to put up with yours too. And there's a cat door in the conservatory. Vasya sleeps out there. Won't they fight over territory?' She pauses, but Janet does not reply. 'I suppose we'll just have to see.' She goes to the door. 'Well, you'll ring then.'

In September Janet moves in with a large wardrobe, a high double bed, two chests inlaid with brass. Kylie helps her unload. Janet shakes a crysanthemum pink duvet out over the bed.

'Oh, that's nice. Cotton.'

'Indian cotton. It was much brighter. It's faded.'

Out of the cat basket onto the faded, autumn pink spread the black and white cat dances. He lifts his legs high. His long, black face with its white flash is high-cheeked and alert. His narrow body coils and sways. Round and round, along and back he prances, whining, over a pink sea stage. The noise is intolerable. A dreadful, winsome, demanding, peevish note repeated and repeated. On and on. Janet ignores him and goes to the van. Kylie, transfixed, leans back against a shelf watching him dance up onto the pillows, up onto the bed ends, down into the crysanthemum swaying pink hollows. Vasya arrives at the door.

Vasya bristles, waiting, eyeing the prancing, whining artiste above her, then advances, transformed into a spiked, grey tabby tank.

'He really is a Sylvester,' Kylie says to Vasya, shocked. Such a spidery-legged, peevish, wailing black and white cat.

Before Vasya reaches the bed Janet returns. Sylvester jumps onto her shoulders and clings while she dumps some books, and is carried quiet and triumphant to the other side of the room.

Which prompts the all-black cat from her all-black, shiny, fur ball wait. The basket door opens over the pink crysanthemum sea. Out onto the soft undulations crawls a black, furry caterpillar cat, slow and frightened.

Suddenly she bounds. A metamorphosed caterpillar cat flies across the room. Vasya, winched up on tabby-tank alert, leaps, too late, onto the bed. Kylie's elbow slips on the shelf against the metal coathangers she brought in for Janet which clatter and crash to the floor. Vasya flees. The black cat, having landed on one of the trunks, takes off again, a furry streak across the stained glass windows, before vanishing on top of Janet's wardrobe. The wardrobe quivers. A heavy, black female cat. Sylvester wails.

'You'll have to stay here,' Janet says to Sylvester, and to Kylie, 'I'll shut them in while I go back to Miranda's.'

Janet is late back that night after returning the van so

Kylie does not see her again until the next morning when Janet strikes it up matey with Bill and the space between the two women begins to starch. They are self-conscious. Although it could be just the newness.

'This will make a noise,' Janet warns, twisting the lid of her coffee grinder. There is a piercing din while she fills the kettle. 'It has to be on quite a while to be fine enough,' she apologies after. 'Would you like some?'

Kylie shakes her head. 'No, thanks. I can't.' She puts a hand on her belly.

'Uumm. Yes. I would,' rumbles Bill. He blinks behind his glasses, his eyes grey-blue, still sleepy, 'I'll try some.'

'You'll try some?' Janet smiles.

Already as familiar as old friends.

Bill grins and brushes off a few oats which have floated from his muesli onto his beard. How nice to have someone else in the house again who isn't preoccupied with work and pregnancy. Someone light-hearted. Kylie heaves herself off upstairs day and night, sighing. He is doing as much as he can to help, building a cradle for her downstairs in the old stable, but there is a limit. And Kylie is so unpredictably moody without Sol around to neutralise things. They are getting on each other's nerves. Though it's always been odd, the initial longing between them which never came to anything, which cast something vaguely erotic around their relationship at first and which seemed to float around again that week Kylie went off and got pregnant. Since then he's found himself starting to hum every time Kylie comes into the kitchen. Tuneless. She hates it, but if he puts up a wall of noise, she puts up a wall of smoke with her cigarettes. Pregnant and smoking. Her risk.

Little by little Janet pours the boiled water over the coffee filter resting on her elegant willow-patterned jug. It sounds like someone pissing. The heavy kitchen door which never shuts properly opens a few inches and there is the black and white cat wailing and winding around Janet's ankles.

'It's Sylvester,' Kylie tells Bill, trying to disguise her horror, to sound cheerful.

'That's not his name really.' Janet puts down the kettle.

Bill looks sleepier and not aghast at all.

Janet takes the coffee to the table and Sylvester jumps onto Bill's dressing-gowned lap. Bill seems to take to it, quite kindly and tolerant as he is despite his dislike of pets, just as he takes to Vasya's curling up on him sometimes when he sits watching TV. Vasya never jumps onto Kylie's knee when they are downstairs together but Kylie refuses to be possessive or jealous about it. Hasn't she given Vasya love, regular feedings, games, hasn't she pulled little balls of paper on string and rippled her fingers mouselike under the carpet, all so Vasya would become an independent and contented little cat, more like a dog than a cat perhaps, and not clinging, bothersome? Vasya never has to stroke and wind round her legs for food. Thank goodness. It would drive her crazy. And wasn't it seeing what a confident animal Vasya turned out to be which gave Kylie the idea of trying it with a baby?

'Vasya? It was after a heroine in a Kollantai novel,' Kylie tells Janet, and Janet describes her work in a little more detail.

'I can't help it. I do like afflicted young men. . . . What is my psychotherapy? Well, I suppose it is behaviourist. Rewards and stuff. There's a dear old man due in tomorrow who can't do anything without washing his hands again and again afterwards.'

Over the next weeks the black, female cat loses weight. Instead of flying onto Janet's wardrobe she scrabbles up. At feeding time, when Janet remembers, she's a shambling caterpillar, Sylvester's thin shadow.

It becomes sensible to feed the three cats together so Janet's concoction is put out onto three saucers in the conservatory which is rather a grand name for the leaking, glassed-in room by the kitchen steps. Once a week the house stinks of the pressure-cooked chicken giblets which Janet prepares to mix with dried cat food. Cheap and it does for a week. Sylvester prances as ever. Vasya spends more and more time upstairs in the daytime, restless because she hates the noise of Kylie's loom and Kylie as usual has to put her on the landing because she jumps onto the yarns.

Kylie notices too that despite the winter, colder nights, Vasya is hardly ever in her box when she goes down in the morning and looks through the window into the conservatory. Sylvester is there instead curled up in Vasya's place. And often no sign of the black cat. So where is Vasya sleeping? It's quite a turn-around because over autumn when the conservatory was still littered with the sticky, deep pink flowers shed by the Busy Lizzie from the hanging basket, Vasya chased the two newcomer cats outside or into Janet's room whenever she had the chance.

Finally before Christmas the baby comes. Bill is helping a friend convert a barn in the Dales, Sol is still away on tour and there is no one but Janet to drive Kylie to hospital because it's all three weeks later than anyone expected and other plans had to be kept to. 'We'll have to induce you,' Dr Horton announces, shaking his head. Another mature prima-gravida who made such a fuss insisting she wanted a homebirth. Might end up a Caesarian too.

Which it does. Kylie quite enjoys the little, pale green room all to herself in St James. Despite her stitches, she seems to be having it easier than some of them in the ward who can hardly walk after their episiotomies. 'Feet first, is that what you wanted,' she laughs in delight at the new little person in her arms. 'We'll be home soon. Such tiny feet. Little Daniel.'

Janet gives baby Daniel a shawl she knitted of light, creamy wool, a sophisticated loose-weave shawl since she started it really as a birthday present for a London friend but never finished it in time. Kylie admires the fringe of blue, maroon, yellow wools.

'They're Italian colours. I chose them after my holiday in Florence last year,' Janet says smiling, holding out a finger to stroke Daniel's tiny head. 'Aah. The fontanelle.'

Kylie is grateful for this gesture though the shawl's weave is just the kind the baby books advise you against since baby's little fingers get caught in it. It would be mean of her to say so and what does it matter, beside Daniel, after all, nothing matters, especially to be home again with him after two weeks in hospital, to be home in time for Christmas.

And Sol is back dancing round all friendliness and concern and they decide to spend Christmas in the house, all of them together, something to do with the baby perhaps bringing them closer, or the snow that year piling up, or the Tories winning the election, whatever, they feel a need to huddle.

Janet spends most mealtimes on the phone. She meets a younger man on her regular seven-thirty train journeys to Manchester. Janet with her little flask of coffee envied by all the other wintry passengers. That was before Daniel was born. The young man is a Bill too so they call him Bill-Manchester when he becomes a regular visitor to differentiate between Bills, and Bill-Manchester tells Janet that her hobby is people, which impresses her and makes her cross. But when Kylie asks, 'Well, do you love him?' she finds her answer is yes.

Kylie feels alone after Christmas in the snow-filled January, such a cocoon January, white, soft time outside and slippery and inside Kylie's shattered, weary beyond speaking of, but one morning in bed after feeding time, Daniel's smiles really begin. Oh, flowering January smiles.

Kylie sits there all morning with him afterwards. After feeding, changing, her breakfast, and watches him asleep in the cradle Bill made. Flowering January wreathes of smiles, ringing around and around. And again, when he wakes later.

'Janet come and see,' she shouts in the evening. Janet does. Then Kylie sits quiet downstairs and waits for dinner. Janet always cooks late and tonight a fruit flan in celebration. Rings of fruit perfectly, glistening, pale green apple.

'It's like a giant Chinese gooseberry,' Kylie exclaims when near midnight it's ready.

'Mmm,' growls Bill, kissing his lips into the air over it. He does that also when he says hello to Janet. 'Mmm,' and the bearded kiss in the air. Kylie finds it hard not to laugh at them both especially when Janet takes to doing it too. Down the hall at each other. 'Helloo. Mmm.' Squeaky, airy kisses.

Nevertheless, nothing matters. Bill holds Daniel's toes and does the airy kisses. Daniel loves it and wreathes up his incomparable baby smiles.

Upstairs while Daniel sleeps Kylie stares from her couch at the white wall, pinkish white in the lamplight, realising Vasya isn't purring as she settles herself beside her, round and round over the black and white ticking stripes, pricking her claws into the cloth. Before Daniel surely Vasya purred every time? And Kylie looks down, her dark eyes puffy with broken nights but glowing, less intense, fiery happy glowing because of Daniel. Vasya is curled and settled but her green-yellow cat eyes are too dark even in the lamplight. Surely they are not usually so empty and sad-looking?

'What is it, Vasya? Are you ill? Oh, I know it's not fair to you. And I don't have time for games now do I? Daniel takes all of my energy.'

Vasya just turns away, her mournful eyes not closing as

usual all comfort-cosy but opening wider, then suddenly she is up. She stretches once. She leaves the couch, leaves the room. Kylie hopes Janet will put Vasya out into the conservatory that night, trusts she will, even though it's all worse in the conservatory amongst the cats. She has no idea where Vasya sleeps anymore. Out the cat door into the night. Somewhere. Sylvester has routed her and Kylie and Janet both know it but say nothing. Instead Janet makes shawls, flans, waters Kylie's palm tree downstairs while Bill carries on letting Sylvester curl on his lap and Sol's not there often enough to notice.

But the next morning when Kylie goes downstairs Janet tells her to sit down, 'I have some bad news.'

Kylie looks at her. Janet's hair is quite wiry and stiff-fair so it stays more or less the same and even in the early morning uncombed it is a flattering blonde-brown nimbus. Janet wraps her dressing-gown tighter around her and frowns, looking worried. Unusual. Kylie without a dressing-gown, in a secondhand striped man's shirt, shivers. The kitchen hasn't warmed up yet and there's frost on the conservatory glass. Kylie's breasts are heavy and ready for the morning feed if only she can have a cup of tea to take upstairs with her.

'Vasya was run over last night. Oh, I blame myself. I know she was being pushed out. Oh, Kylie, I'm so sorry. I'm so sorry.'

Guilt mars Janet's face, clouding the blue-green eyes. So calm, cool.

'No. No. It's not your fault. Oh, dear. Poor Vasya. Something was up. I knew, last night.' Daniel begins to cry upstairs. No time to mourn Vasya now.

'How did you know?' Puzzled.

'She gave me such a strange look, almost as if she was saying goodbye. Last night. I thought she was getting ill or something. I have felt bad about neglecting her since Daniel.'

'Bill found her when he was going home. He'd decided to leave because of some meeting early this morning. She was in the snow at the side of the road. It looked as if a car skidded on the ice. It must have been quick. Oh, I am sorry. I wondered whether to wake you but I know you need all the sleep you can get.'

The two Bills bury her that night, digging away the snow first, by the pear tree out the back, and Kylie never sees the dead body.

To Sol later Kylie cries, 'She knew. She knew she was going to die. And I tried to talk to Janet about the cats' territory but she didn't want to think about it and I couldn't cope either, I'm so busy with Daniel and everything. Oh, dear.' She sobs and never forgets the look on Vasya's greyish tabby face, her beautiful black mask lines stretching back from her nose to her ears, her greyish sweet tabby coat.

Then the snow turns to slush and mud but spring comes and the garden zings into spring life. The blackberry-gooseberry tangle lights up with tiny, pale-luminous leaves. And the pear tree in white blossom. Sol on a brief visit home picks some to decorate the dinner table one night celebrating Daniel's first real meal, a sieved banana, but the heavy, budding branches topple and Sylvester, on Bill's lap as so often, screeches and claws Bill's beard. Janet pretends to be cross with him, takes him to her room and shuts him in.

'I was dreadful with those cats,' she confesses when she comes back. 'When I got them in London I was quite depressed and lonely. It was a miserable time. And every night when I came home from work I lavished attention on them. Then things changed and I didn't have so much time for them.' She shakes her head. Too obvious to everyone to say more.

In spring too the retiring all black female cat takes to disappearing. Bill discovers her new hideout. She has found a way into the stable downstairs through a hole in the door where the wood is damp and rotting. There she perches on top of an old post, quiet and shambly, still as a sitting ghost, a black and yellow-eyed scaredy-cat. She loses more weight. Her fur dulls but she appears scraggy upstairs for meals and eats quickly. Sylvester wails and dances around, a warrior cat competing in yells with Daniel who begins to have regular meals in a dish, who dribbles his food in gay abandon and lies on a rug on the floor pushing his arms and legs out imitating a crawler, practising, and just after he pushes his body along on his first proper crawl, the second cat death.

There is a terrible, terrible din from the bottom of the garden. Nine months since Janet moved in. Packs of dogs a great nuisance unless you know one or two, like Churchill next door who is all bark and only a little bite, but if some of the Alsations get together! Not only gardens grow wild in this street. The dogs a problem and Kylie fearful of them for later because she reads in the paper that the number of dog-bitten young children is increasing. They keep the gate closed at the bottom of the drive. Who left it open? Torn apart, down by the drive, the soft, scraggy, all-black she-cat, mauled bloody, to death, by the dogs. In play. In practice. In nature. In retribution, Kylie feels awful, thinking that. It serves Janet right, letting Sylvester screech and forcing Vasya out into the cold and not caring that that poor black cat was such a neurotic, dying creature anyway. Foredoomed a victim. Not Janet's fault at all. What is she thinking about? These dreadful thoughts, and Janet's been so kind to her and they get on fine, especially given that Janet said right at the beginning she wouldn't describe herself as a feminist, though that began to change, and finding Janet admirable, the way she is her-own-woman, so floating decisive about what she wants, always late, always with time enough.

After that the collective, just about viable, comes to the

end of its viability. Janet buys a house with her Bill-Manchester who of course likes Sylvester. Kylie moves to another woman friend's who also has a baby. Sol and Bill take off for Montreal where Sol gets work in a show called *Only Men* and Bill writes to Kylie about a men's massage group which was 'amazing', during which he found he could see without his glasses. Unfortunately it was only ten minutes before his short-sightedness came back.

A year or so later Janet tells Kylie she too is pregnant. Kylie, reading Anaïs Nin, finds something she thinks Janet might appreciate and copies it out for her:

> When Renate's cat died of a snake bite I told her what I had heard from the Haitians: 'Be glad, as it takes the curse off the house and family. They say that cats often deflect misfortune.'*

And so it goes. Janet likes the quote. Definitely it was a chancy winter. They, both the women, know that.

The Journals of Anaïs Nin, Volume Six 1955-1966, Quartet Books, London, 1979, page 35.

SINCE AGNES LEFT

Jackie Kay

Nobody's ever made me feel like this before. I never believed the edge of aloneness could be cut away so gently. Makes me able to imagine a forever, stretching out ahead of us, solid land we can walk together. Makes me able to imagine a forever.

She wandered around her small garden in her slippers. The ground beneath her was hard and ungiving. No flowers to tend to. The roses, dramatically drab in this winter morning, waited for summer. She threw some stale bread on the frozen grass for the birds. Poor things, it was a hard winter for them too. She inhaled her breath in sharp staccato rhythm and blew out visible signs.

Back inside her small council house, she put the kettle on and moved slowly towards her window. She watched the sparrows feast. Her eyes shifted their slow gaze onto the sky as she contemplated that peculiar light travelling westwards. This kind of winter morning troubled her.

The kettle's whistle interrupted, startling her into activity. She put some boiling water in the tea-pot to warm it, swirled the water around the bottom and threw it in the sink. As she measured the tea in the palm of her hand, her mind grasped at memories. The times she had done exactly the same thing: Agnes and she had sat down to one last cup of well-brewed tea before she had left. The tea then had tasted the way it always tasted and she couldn't understand it.

Placing her bright woollen tea-cosy on the pot, she laid it on the table and sat down waiting for the tea to brew. Her short, thick fingers tapped the solid oak table, calling memory back. She poured herself a mug, she always used the same mug, the one with the pink flamingoes, that Agnes had bought her ten years ago. It pleased her that it had acquired no chips over the years. Sipping the hot comforting tea, she wondered, if someone were standing just outside my window, what would they see? She had no idea where such a thought came from, but she saw as clearly as if she were standing outside of herself the visible reply. A woman past fifty answered her. Deep and dark, her eyes looked as if once you went into them, you would never return. Her cheeks were black with an orange-red glow like the high lights in a fire. She had that fresh look of someone often outside in the tough winter air, but her skin was not dry; she had evidently rubbed cocoa butter into her cheeks over the years. A bold red and turquoise scarf covered her tight curls. Her legs sat solidly apart. Her arms, you could tell she liked those arms, they had carried a thing or two: the weights, the wood, the babies that had all been held in those plump strong arms.

She knew it was time now to carry some more things. She was aware that she had been putting it off and it wasn't like Beulah Wilson to stall – no, it was Agnes whose middle name was hesitation. She rose, this time with alacrity, and went into her boudoir, as Agnes had called it. Standing in front of the old Victorian dresser that they had bought out of a second-hand furniture shop twelve years ago, she opened the top drawer. With purpose, she headed back to her kitchen, holding on to her treasure for grim life. She laid each one down on the oak table which she had made herself.

Beulah was always remembering the story to her table. Agnes and she had been coming home one Saturday.

Beulah had noticed this skip outside someone's house. She had stopped walking and stared. Agnes had been embarrassed at her gazing into rubbish in broad daylight out in the street. But the huge piece of oak had caught her eye. Beulah, after some heated discussion, persuaded Agnes to help her carry the top home. After a few weeks she cut it down to the size she wanted, stripped it, and then, working with her favourite tool, her wood Jack Plane, reduced the thickness, planing with the close grain and smoothing the surface. She didn't re-varnish it because she liked the dullness of the bare wood. From a timber shop in town she'd bought some pine wood to make the legs; oak was too expensive. She stained them till they nearly matched the colour of the oak. So she had the kitchen table she'd dreamed of, the most wonderful table in the world, since she had made it herself. Agnes had been so impressed and called her *my handy woman* for ages afterwards. Beulah chuckled to herself, pleased with the memory.

Chopping wood was one activity that never changed. Beulah had chopped wood in her small back garden for years now. She had her own particular axe – an old-fashioned one with a heavy wood handle. It was hard work but she enjoyed the sweat rhythm and you could always find a use for wood. She loved the curls that fell off the wood when she was planing it and the sawdust that scattered when she was sanding. And she loved the grain. Although Agnes shared her affection for wood, she never made anything with it, or chopped it. She had accompanied Beulah to second-hand furniture shops though, and spent hours touching and looking. There wasn't one such shop in St Albans that they hadn't visited. They knew which shop was best for wardrobes, which kept desks in good condition, which often had one-off surprises, like the one where they had found the lovely old milking-stool that sat in their kitchen.

Beulah remembered the shop where they had bought the dresser. The man in there had kept trying to ascertain whether there would be a man at the other end to help with the delivery. Beulah and Agnes had said a simultaneous 'No'. 'I promise you, I'm as strong as any man,' Beulah had said in what Agnes called her no-nonsense voice. 'Okay dear,' the man had replied regarding them both speculatively. Beulah had wondered then, as she often wondered, how many people guessed what their relationship was. No doubt many considered them sisters, even though they didn't look a bit alike.

Agnes was taller than Beulah and younger by seven years. She dressed with style and her face was often dramatically made up. Her hair was thick and straightened, her skin, lighter than Beulah's, a sort of cinnamon brown. She loved dancing and listening to music and her expressions conveyed her passion for life. Agnes was mad about music, especially jazz. Some people thought she looked like Sarah Vaughan and Agnes was delighted at the comparison; she repeated it at every opportunity. Perhaps it was the way she walked that people really noticed. Beulah was struck by the way Agnes carried herself from the beginning.

Beulah was getting impatient with herself. She had to get on. She had things to do. All these memories, jumbled as a junk shop, were interfering with her concentration. To that someone peering in at the window, Beulah's eyes held a fascinating glint. You might return from those eyes; they were going somewhere. Her jaw loosening up, that set expression of something that could have only approached defeat was waning. Her face was full of movement now; her chest rose and fell; her breathing was excited and irregular. Her feet in her fluffy slippers tapped the rug on the floor.

It was, she knew, although she hadn't been totally conscious of it the past few days, almost two years since

Agnes left. She wasn't sure of the date, but she remembered the month and the morning. January 1983. Agnes and she had been together then for a full ten years. Beulah had been talking of that at the end of the year; she had kept saying, 'Just think Agnes – a decade!' Shortly after that Agnes had been strange. Beulah hadn't thought much about it at first; Agnes snapped in and out of moods as quickly as she changed her clothes. In the beginning, Beulah had hated those quick-silver moods because they stole her certainty. As their friendship developed, she learnt to recognise Agnes's signals and became less afraid of her anger; she knew what to expect. There were always raging explosions with plenty of interjections of Agnes's favourite emotional words and expressions like *What on earth!* (the assumption being that Agnes's earth and Beulah's were on two different planets) *What on earth do you expect me to do!* (and *expect* was always said in such a way that made Beulah feel her expectations were simply outlandish) or *Damn it Beulah!* or *If that's the way it's going to be.* This last one never failed, Beulah always replied, 'No, no it's not Agnes'. And then there were the short effective words like *Blast, Lord* and *Mercy.* After the chosen outburst, Agnes would be fairly quiet and a mixture of shame and pride would rest on those lovely cheeks. It took Beulah quite a while to realise that Agnes enjoyed exploding, that she wasn't always completely serious. Sometimes she'd have a wry look on her face totally aware of what she was doing, her private smile to herself. Beulah thought it was as if Agnes was performing, not that her script was untruthful, simply that she was standing outside watching herself and chuckling, challenging Beulah to see through her. And Beulah did. Sometimes that annoyed her even although she had encouraged Beulah to look beyond. If Agnes were silently fuming, Beulah knew it was more dangerous. She knew not to ask what the matter was. She had heard too many curt 'Nothings' for that. Nothing was such a full word sometimes. So she would be still whilst Agnes read or listened to her music, waiting for her to confide her worry. Beulah always knew instantly if something was wrong; Agnes's face told a story.

This was what flummuxed Beulah that January two years ago. Agnes was different. She wasn't in one of her quick-silver moods. Something serious was bothering her and for the first time in years Beulah hadn't a clue what it could be. Agnes just had this air of impatience and irritation. She'd snap at her for little reason. After a week of this, Beulah did ask what the matter was. For once Agnes did not say *Nothing*. (How she wished for that curt word back.)

Agnes had seemed relieved at the question. She had picked up Beulah's hand and held it the whole time they talked. Beulah's hand went numb and then got cramp; the tingling pain gave her some other focus. Agnes had said some very confusing things to her. They had sat up talking till three in the morning which was unusual for Beulah since she was an early to bed, early to rise woman. At least, Agnes had talked mostly and she had listened with wide incredulous ears.

The next morning was a Saturday, Beulah remembered it in minute detail: she had risen at the same time that she usually rose on Saturday mornings, eight o'clock, tired but pleased to get up. She thought of the night before as she put the kettle on. Already it had acquired an unreal quality. It was morning now, she listened to the morning sounds and watched the light in the sky shift westwards. She went out to her garden and walked briskly breathing in the ice-cold air. Usually, she treasured these Saturday mornings, this time to herself with the weekend lying deliciously ahead of her, whilst Agnes lay still oblivious to the world and its movements until nine, sometimes ten. This morning it was misty, that clear winter morning mist that does not really obscure vision. She went back into her kitchen answering the whistle of the kettle, feeling troubled but better. Last night was surely a nightmare the morning sang. There was nothing like the daytime to return sensible proportions to thoughts. Last night she had believed it was over between them, tossing with the awful thought in a state that was neither sleep nor consciousness.

When Agnes rose a few hours later, the mist had cleared completely; the light was far up in the sky. Beulah knew by the look in Agnes's eyes that she ought to have trusted in the night and started preparing herself for this.

It was ten in the morning. Beulah could not allow herself to prevaricate any longer. The woman outside the window noticed those plump hands unclasp themselves. She wondered what Beulah was going to do. The woman was cold standing outside peering in. She rubbed her hands as she watched Beulah get up and walk to her fireplace. Beulah bent down and rolled the newspaper, which lay by the fire, into tight cones. She placed them criss cross on the grate. Then she put some dry twigs on top. She set them alight, her eyes captured by the sudden burst of flames. When the fire had truly caught she put some substantial logs on top. She was drawn to real fires, the bright varying colours, the crackling and struggling noises, the force behind the flames and the direct heat that came after a while like an additional present.

She realised how cold she had been feeling. Her toes inside her slippers were tingling numb; a persistent shiver travelled the length of her back. Usually she lit the fire as soon as she got up. She stood enraptured by the capricious colours and the sparks jolted her towards her task. She returned to her oak table and special chair with the semi-circle back and crocheted cushion cover. She sat down. Ready now. She had five special pieces of her life to uncover. Without hesitation, she unwrapped the brown paper around her first memory.

Agnes's voice sang to her, *Just one look at you and my heart goes tipsy/You and you alone bring out the gipsy in me.* The photograph was taken in 1974 after they had been in love for an entire year. It was framed, a plain dark wood frame. They were standing in front of the red-bricked council house. Agnes had her arm round Beulah and was fondly gazing into her eyes with a look that said naughtily, *After this click, let's go to bed.* Mr Jamieson next door, who was taking this image for posterity, must have noticed the look. He was never as friendly or as nosey after that. The innocent spinsters next door had turned into something else. He kept his wife away from them too. He must have heard it could be catching.

Beulah fingered the rectangular frame. Agnes looked so good in that picture. She was wearing her wool coat with a checkered scarf around her neck. The photograph held them in black and white. It must have been taken in the winter. Beulah remembered the day well. Agnes had been quite besotted with her. She had kept singing to her, *It's crazy, but I'm in love.* They had danced together in the living room, a sort of rumba that Agnes had taught her – the base for every dancing foot she had called it. Beulah danced rhythmically moving her hips thinking in between beats, if my mother could see me now. They had eaten out that night. Agnes had insisted on it. In the small Italian restaurant, they ate splendidly and drank el vino, as Agnes called it. Beulah sipped it tentatively. She loved Agnes that night, her carefreeness, her boldness, her imagination; she treasured the world that Agnes gave her.

You know something Beulah? You are some woman. We are so good together. Who would have dreamt us up? There is nothing like loving – it beats a good book, a satisfying job! There is nothing like loving. You know what I really liked about you from the beginning? Your eyes, that gaze of yours holds me, makes me feel safe, the intensity of the darkness.

Beulah felt confused now. Today was the first time that she could remember thinking about Agnes with affection since they had parted. That morning Agnes had drunk her tea as usual and smoked her cigarette. She had looked so miserable, even Beulah could see that. *I am sorry Beulah, so sorry. I never wanted to hurt you. I love you. I will always love, you, but in a different way. You have to believe me.* How could she say that? Love me and leave me? It didn't make sense. Beulah had kept her thoughts to herself. Agnes had seen them register on her face and said simply. *Maybe one day you will know why I had to go.* Beulah had nodded thinking, Never.

Agnes had started packing that same morning. She said once you decide to go you have to go. Beulah didn't recognise this sharp woman with purpose and direction, this lover of hers who had slept in her bed for ten years, and at last knew where she was going. Agnes had always been the one who was unsure about what she wanted from life. She changed her mind just about every week in the entire ten years. The things Beulah had seen her become, the imaginings she had shared with her, the mountain of wild ideas that came tumbling down regularly. *I want to learn to play jazz piano/the saxophone/the trumpet/maybe we could set up an antique shop with a cafe in the back serving ground coffee and cakes/run a holiday home for middle-life women like ourselves/go and live in Paris.* But the money for all of these ideas was never forthcoming and Beulah was rather glad it wasn't.

Beulah was a midwife. She felt settled in her job. She enjoyed it because she felt she was doing something valuable. It didn't pay enough to finance Agnes's fantasia.

Agnes worked as a receptionist at the local health clinic where they had first met. Beulah had been on a visit to the clinic. She noticed this tallish black woman standing at the reception staring at her unflinchingly. She had felt quite embarrassed. She smiled a little in acknowledgment, but that didn't stop the woman staring. She was a beautiful-looking woman. Beulah noticed her posture right away; she admired women who held themselves well. The woman's deep imaginative eyes watched whilst she appraised her. This woman knew how to dress too! Beulah always envied women who wore their clothes as if the had been specially made for them. No matter what she wore she always felt slightly out of sorts with her body. This woman was a picture of elegant ease, dressed in a stylish suit whose burgundy colour reflected the glow in her high-boned cheeks. She wore a delicate cream blouse under the jacket. Beulah just had to say hello. She approached her and in her most polite voice said, *How do you do?* For years Agnes teased her about that first meeting. She had said Beulah was a brash woman striding up to a complete stranger and saying *How do you do?* in so polite a voice that it seemed an ordinary, civil thing to do. Beulah maintained it was, especially if someone was staring at you, but she smiled each time Agnes imitated her just the same.

Beulah unwrapped the linen cloth around her second memory. Inside lay a rectangular wooden box. A small key was wrapped in another piece of cloth. Before she turned it, she laid her hands on her box. How she'd missed that box! It was made from yellow birch and had little triangular pieces of walnut inset on the lid. Each side had one small triangle inlaid too. The box was smooth, so smooth it soothed her to stroke it. She remembered the last time she had touched her box. She had put it in the top drawer of her dresser with all the other things. It was two weeks after Agnes had left. The postman had brought her a letter in Agnes's handwriting. She had opened it eagerly wishing with all her might that she had changed her mind and was coming back to her. She had scanned the letter and not finding in it what she wanted, placed it in her box, and put the box in her dresser out of sight. She had felt in a whirl of rage. How dare she, that Agnes, desert her and the home that they had carefully built up over the years without so much as a sensible explanation!

Beulah had looked in the mirror on the dresser. *Why did she go and leave me?* Already the two weeks felt like an age; they had never been separated this long for the whole time that they were together. *Maybe she didn't like this dark hair around my mouth?* No, that couldn't be right, she remembered Agnes saying hair wouldn't be anywhere it wasn't supposed to be. Why? After all those years? She'd gone forever. For always. The house knew she'd left, the emptiness hung in the very air of it. But, she had been able to see the years stretch themselves into old age. *Who will I grow old with now, Agnes?* And then the anger again: *how dare you leave me this way?* She was angry at herself too: all those mornings and evenings together; how many mornings were there in ten years? And yet, she hadn't foreseen this end. She hadn't pictured Beulah Wilson standing here, solitariness so painfully drawn in the very attitude. Her shoulders knew aloneness now.

You look like you could do with a good rub. Where is the cocoa butter? Let me loosen those knots. You must have had a hard day.

That hurts.

You'll feel the benefit later, my love.

How long since she had been massaged that way? *Agnes. Who is going to get the benefit of those healing hands now?*

The rage had quickly spun itself into a state of exhaustion and then developed into a deep and dangerous self-pity. Feeling so sorry for herself, Beulah avoided even remembering accurately. All of her energy went towards this pity, a pity that sucked in her cheeks and shut out the sparkle from her eyes. Through these eyes, the eyes that had been betrayed and deserted, she went back over their ten years together, reconstructing their entire relationship and seeing Agnes in the most distorted light. Agnes was mad. Beulah supposed she had always known that. Now it was absolutely obvious. Agnes had sensed that Beulah knew and that's why she left. She had become too much of an expert at anticipating Agnes's little games. In fact, their whole relationship had been one long game for Agnes. No, she had never really loved her. She had treated her so badly it didn't bear thinking. She had used her. All that time and Agnes was really thinking this or that. Beulah shut herself inside these buildings haunted with fake memories, adding more and more, piling them up. At work, at home, walking down the street, or doing her shopping, she'd suddenly think of another one and suck in her cheeks saying, 'That's right, I'd forgotten about that.'

What is it that you want me to do? Declare that we will be together forever? I can't do that Beulah.

I remember you mentioning a forever once Agnes.

Don't throw things back in my face, that was then. I feel different now.

About me? You don't love me anymore?

No, not about you, about myself.

That was a game too. People should learn not to make promises they can't keep. The hurt of the let-down. She had said forever and she had meant it then. So it must be her feelings towards her that changed. What nonsense —

'about myself'. *She just couldn't have felt like I've felt all along. Otherwise she'd be here with me.* It was as simple as that. Everything else was a game. She sucked in her cheeks again. Strangely, it gave her a grim pleasure, being sure of her own feelings, knowing that she was the one who knew the meaning of the word promise, or trust, or forever.

Yet even as Beulah constructed these painfully satisfying memories, she had missed Agnes. Each day of the past two years, she had lived with an unbearable consciousness of this massive loss in her life. She went about her daily business with little energy. Her few friends wondered and worried, and perhaps some guessed, but no one dared to talk about Agnes with her. So she missed alone, having no one to sympathise with her or listen to her. Agnes and she had always been private in the town. If people knew, they pretended not to, and that is how they all got along. Beulah missed alone. She would not be humoured by any friend's see-through efforts or offers out to the cinema. She didn't want charity. She had told that to Elspeth, her closest friend. It never occured to her to think that Elspeth might want her company, might welcome the opportunity to have some time alone, without Agnes. In any case, she felt emptied of any potential to love or to care.

Beulah heard some sentences that Agnes had said that night over and over. They hung out in her memory, stranded and desperate, repeating themselves in Agnes's low voice; they were like a record on a gramophone that some mechanical hand insisted on turning around and around. *Beulah, I don't think our relationship is going anywhere anymore. Beulah, I don't think our relationship is going anywhere anymore. Beulah, Beulah, Beulah.*

Beulah turned the key to her precious wooden box. Agnes had found it in one of their antique shops and hidden it until Beulah's forty-fifth birthday. They had spent nearly four years together then. Agnes gave it to her wrapped in bright emerald green paper with a purple bow stuck on top. She unwrapped it eagerly and fell in love with the box straight away. It was the perfect present for her. Inside lay a little note on lilac paper:

For Beulah, November 7th 1978.
Every time you open this little wooden box, think of me and our love for each other. Keep your treasures in your miniature chest, my love. I will treasure you always.
Agnes xxx

The note was still intact along with the letter that Agnes had sent her in February 1983. She had kept all the notes and letters from Agnes in her wooden box. To treasure. But, she tapped her feet on the rug again, it wasn't her purpose to sit here maudlin and read them all. No, it was just the last one that concerned her.

The woman outside was beginning to feel like an intruder. But she knew she had to stay till it was over. She had to see it through. She was glad of her warm winter coat and her fur-lined boots. She wished she had remembered her gloves. She rubbed her hands again, gazing longingly at that log fire. Beulah had at last taken off her gardening coat and her bright scarf. She had looked such an incongrous mixture, sitting in her kitchen with her shabby coat, bright scarf and fluffy slippers. Her hair was sparkled with silver gray, her curls tightly packed into her neck. Her face looked softer now and the handsomeness of her broad features ventured forth after two years in hibernation.

The woman's eyes focused on the letter held in Beulah's hand. She couldn't make out the writing; she didn't want to anyway. She just knew she had to be there when Beulah was ready. Her hand was steady holding the letter. Her eyes stuck to Agnes' large and erratic characters. She read it as if for the first time.

February 2nd 1983

My dear Beulah,

I can imagine what you must be feeling right now, and believe me it hurts, picturing you by the fire, in the bedroom, in the garden, unhappy and wretched. You must trust me when I say I never intended to hurt you. I tried to talk with you that awful night, but I don't think you heard what I was saying. Please let me try again Beulah and tell you briefly the reasons I had to leave.

For some time before we talked, I felt trapped in our relationship. I felt like I would never be able to grow up as long as I had you. I am forty-four now Beulah. I have to be able to stand on my own. There are things I want to try. I'm not sure if I'll succeed, but I must try. I know that you are thinking you wouldn't stop me from doing anything I wanted. But I would stop myself. I would wrap myself up in your protective indulgence. I became too dependent on you and you didn't even notice. You are happy with your work and your home. You are settled inside, Beulah. I am not. Nor have I ever been. I have to find some security within myself. I was getting irritated trying this and that and having ideas that never materialised.

Beulah, I don't think I am good for you anymore. (I can hear you saying, 'Let me be the one to decide that!') But for once I had to decide something. I think I played too many tricks on you and myself. You must know what I mean. I often tried to get you to reject me, but you knew me too well for that. You wouldn't allow it. So I had to be the deserter and risk losing it all.

I just couldn't have gone on like that for the rest of my life. The routine that you find so satisfying – you chopping wood, me cooking dinner, both of us shopping together, all the little habits that we became enmeshed in.

I had to leave before I could break them.

You won't possibly be able to imagine how hard it will be for me to adjust to not being in our little nest. I am missing you so much already. I'm scared of being lonely too. It would have been much easier to stay, settled in our day-to-dayness. You would always get home from work later than me. I would usually have something cooking. You would always rise earlier than me, and always bring me a cup of tea. I'm not saying I didn't love it Beulah, or that I found it boring, but there was beginning to be something too safe about it. It was delicious, and I cherished the times we had together, but everything must change. Is that why you don't like the song?

I want you to know that you are precious to me. I have learnt so much from you. You gave me some belief in myself. You are the first person I have ever met who didn't accept the surface I presented as me. Our love gave me such confidence. But I had to leave before it turned sour. We gave each other what we could Beulah, if we are to give any more our relationship has to change.

I want us to try this Beulah. We are too important to each other just to disappear out of each other's lives. Please let us be friends, not lovers, and continue seeing each other regularly. When you feel ready for this, I'll be waiting.

I can't tell you how sorry I am for the pain I'm causing you. It is not your fault Beulah. I love you so much and won't stop loving you. My address is on the envelope, please write to me soon. Please forgive me someday, and take care of yourself meanwhile.

Lovingly,
Agnes xxx

Beulah was sobbing now. Her large shoulders moved up and down, carrying her pain in fits and starts. *Oh Agnes* she kept saying *Oh Agnes*. The tears rushed down her cheeks and her pores seemed to open up to drink the drops of salty water. These were the first tears she had parted with since Agnes left. It had been sore holding them in, close to her chest. Her body tensed and relaxed, letting each memory come fully in to let the pain out. With each stuttering breath, she drew in another *Agnes. Agnes. Where are you now?*

The times she used to be sitting on the opposite chair, reading or listening to her music. The times they had kissed hello and goodbye. She could just about visualise them holding each other in the kitchen with the curtains drawn in the evening. The times they had slept in that big old bed, close to each other, even in dreams. *Where does forever go when you can no longer imagine it?* She remembered the look on Agnes's face when she left. Then, she hadn't really wanted to see her pain. She had come up to her after the laborious packing had finished. All the joint possessions, she had decided to leave behind. *You are leaving us behind.* The dresser hurt now and the milking stool. She tied the last strap. Only the taxi to wait for now. *This is the beginning of the waiting.* She came up to her at last when the taxi driver sounded his horn.

Well Beulah . . .

There is nothing left to say.

Agnes clumsily kissed her unwilling cheeks goodbye. She left without another word. Beulah listened to the sound of the taxi pulling away. *So different from all the other kisses goodbye.* This one could last forever. Maybe that was where forever had gone, with Agnes, since she left.

Yes. That was what she had missed most of all, her best friend had gone. No one to complain with, to say simply, 'Did you read that in the paper today?' or 'Aren't the flowers in the garden doing themselves proud?' or 'What do you think of . . . ?' No one to ask, 'How do I look in this dress?' Now and again she wanted to talk instinctively into Agnes's listening ears.

She picked out from her box her fourth memory. It was wrapped in cotton wool. The solid silver ring with the shiny black onyx stone. She remembered now what Agnes had said when she gave it to her. It was the autumn of 1982. They had been out for a walk that day, breathing in the rust oranges and yellows and the brisk sunshine of the autumn day. They walked arm in arm, happy to be with each other out of doors. They relished the colours; it was almost as if the leaves were changing before their very eyes. That night Agnes cooked a delicious lasagna and after they had eaten she gave Beulah the present. It was their ninth anniversary. Beulah had managed to get the date wrong again. She always forgot it or got it wrong right up to their tenth year, and then she had been absolutely jubilant at getting it right. Beulah loved the ring and wore it on the middle finger of her left hand. It suited her so much. She felt that at last she had something that looked as if it had been specially made for her. Agnes had said, and these were the words Beulah had forgotten, *Even if we ever part Beulah, please keep this ring and wear it as a witness to our long and rich friendship.* Beulah had thought it a melodramatic thing to say, and dismissed it as belonging to Agnes's world of dreams. She hadn't promised, because the idea, were she to take it seriously, frightened her. So she had laughed it off. Agnes had looked hurt and Beulah supposed it was because she had forgotten their anniversary again.

That night, before Agnes left, Beulah remembered her saying, *Don't forget the good times Beulah.* She had asked Agnes why the good times had to stop, why she was talking all this leaving rubbish. Agnes had become angry then, and said she was leaving because she was bored. Bored. That was the word she had used. Beulah's expression must have scared Agnes because in an instant she was all over her saying, *I didn't mean it Beulah, honestly I didn't. You just keep making me feel guilty.*

Her sobbing had stopped. She put the ring on her finger and the letter back in the box. She locked it and put it on the mantelpiece. This was where it would sit now. It used to sit on the dresser in the bedroom, but she couldn't put it back in the same place. Some things had to change around here.

She rose and put on the kettle. She was thirsty and hungry and knew that the woman outside would be too. She'd been aware of her presence all morning. It was as if she was in the background of a dream. It had comforted her, some other soul out there whilst she sobbed the morning away. She went to the door and opened it. She had been crying too. She wasn't surprised that Beulah knew she was there, just anxious in case Beulah was cross with her.

'Elspeth,' Beulah said, 'come on in.' Elspeth came into the kitchen, chittering with the cold. 'Sit down Elspeth,' Beulah invited as she put the tea pot on the table. She poured each of them a cup of tea. 'Thanks,' Elspeth said, sipping the warmth slowly, letting it slide down her throat and into her stomach. Feeling a little better, she looked up at Beulah who was looking at her. 'Beulah?' Beulah's eyes said 'Yes.' 'We've been so worried about you. We just didn't know what you might do to yourself.' Elspeth looked as if she could mention endless possibilities of what damage Beulah could have done, but Beulah interrupted: 'I know Elspeth, I've been quite selfish. I realised that this morning. So many things fell into place this morning, after all this time.' She looked to see if Elspeth's face carried any understanding. Seeing what she was looking for, she changed course: 'One thing I can't understand is why you were standing out there in the cold for so long without so much as a knock on the door, or a you who I'm here.'

Elspeth looked slightly guilty. 'I saw you yesterday at

the shops. You didn't even notice me. The last few times that I've been around here, I've felt you were hardly aware of me. I mean before you were numb but conscious, quite officious or something, just getting on, making ends meet. But in the last few weeks, I've noticed a change in you, and it worries me; I thought you were going to snap. I wanted to come round last night, remember, I phoned?'

'Oh yes,' Beulah said doubtfully.

'And you didn't sound like you wanted to see me. So I came round this morning instead. But when I arrived I looked in at your window and you looked straight back at me, or through me, anyway you didn't seem to see me at all. And you had this look on your face. I don't know, somehow I didn't feel that I could disturb you. But I didn't want to leave you either, so I waited.'

Beulah looked slightly pleased at all this. But something was still bothering her. 'Yes, I can understand that. But why did you come in the first place?' Elspeth looked shocked; she thought perhaps that Beulah hadn't heard a word she'd said. 'Why did I come?' she echoed, 'Oh Beulah, don't be daft, I came because I care for you, because we are friends. You must know that by now. I know how lonely and miserable you've been the past couple of years without Agnes; I've tried and tried to talk with you about her, but you just wouldn't or couldn't. I didn't understand it, I thought it would help talking with someone. Anyway, I knew that sometime you would be ready and I'd be here, that's all.'

'So you knew about Agnes and me then?'

'Of course.'

Beulah tried to disguise her surprise thinking to herself how foolish she had been. She thought now that no love as intense as theirs could stay private if people knew that it was possible. And they had prided themselves on being so discreet. It struck her as a huge joke. She wished she could tell Agnes about it. She wanted to laugh out loud at the notion that their old friend Elspeth had known all of these years and never said a word to them about it. Instead she asked Elspeth, 'Have you ever seen Agnes since she left?'

Elspeth looked puzzled, 'Why do you ask that?'

'Oh, I just thought she might have asked you to keep an eye out for me, that's all.'

'No, I've never seen her. Listen Beulah, you are my friend. We've known each other for years, longer even than you and Agnes were together. Agnes never really had any friends of her own here did she?'

Beulah thought for a minute. 'No, no, I suppose she didn't.'

'What are you going to do now Beulah? You've been off sick for two weeks and I don't think . . . '

'I know. I'll start back at work next week. I'll start back in the world. I might even drop Agnes a line and tell her I'm not dying anymore. Maybe she'll still be in London at the same address.' Beulah looked at Elspeth and smiled, 'Do you mind if I play you my fifth memory?'

'No. Not at all. I'd be honoured,' Elspeth replied, enjoying catching a glimpse of the old Beulah.

Beulah looked at the cover of the Sarah Vaughan album. Sarah looked stunning and sad in a photograph that must have been taken in the fifties. The depth of expression in her eyes reminded her of Agnes when she was singing the Blues to her. She took the album out of its cover and put it on the record player. She put the needle on the particular track she wanted and sat down again. 'Now, I'm remembering it all.' Elspeth smiled at Beulah pensively as they listened to Sarah sing, in a voice that crossed the country of their imagination and travelled the pain of their pasts. She sang: *In this world of overrated pleasure, of underrated treasures, I'm glad there is you.*

STRANGERS

Moy McCrory

The only time that I met Aileen McNaughton was on a terrible wet day in a month that felt like February. It was foul, miserable weather. I had recently had my hair permed in a dingy hairdresser's shop, one of those strange little businesses that are hidden away inside old buildings in Belfast's centre. To get to them the customer must walk up two or three flights of stairs past all manner of name plates on doors that are always locked. The stairs are never swept and the light bulbs never work or have been stolen from the sockets. Oddly furtive little places that you know you will never find again. My hair turned into a mass of springy curls and being much thicker in those days it became impossible to manage. I swear that it was the following Christmas before I could get a comb through it. When a friend finally cut the curls from me in her kitchen one night they lay on the newspaper at my feet in perfect little corkscrews, defiant to the last.

As I said, it was a terrible wet day and my hair clung to my head in tight permed curls when I arrived in the village where Aileen grew up. It was early on Saturday morning. I had left my house while still dark and caught the first Ulsterbus from Oxford Street station. Although the sky lightened as the morning drew on, there was no sign of the rain becoming less insistent. When I stepped down from that bus I did not know of Aileen's existence. My reason to be in her home place was on account of a friend who had moved there from the city. I was going to spend a weekend with her in what I hoped would be a retreat.

I found the row of houses without too much difficulty by following Shelagh's description. She had told me to look out for a tall grey stone building at the end of the row that turned towards the street and stood higher than the rest of the cottages backed crookedly against its gable end. I walked down past it and was in the narrow cul de sac that ran behind and outside her door in a matter of minutes.

'Jesus!' she said as soon as she saw me, 'that perm's an innovation. God Almighty, it's as if someone's stuck black pipe cleaners all over your skull.'

Shelagh usually said the first thing that came into her head and, depending on who it was, would then spend the rest of her time apologising. She knew me too well to have to bother but it reminds me that I had no grey then and I remember that I was certainly rosier, plumper and better able to swallow Guinness. I apparently never worried about how I might feel the next morning because I always rose like clockwork, healthy, fighting fit and ready to take on whatever the day had in store for me, until I became the insomniac of now. Sleepless nights have a way of dulling the keenest enthusiasm. I suppose in those days I never thought that I could ever have trouble sleeping.

'Haven't you chosen a great weekend to come down? Jesus, you had your pick and look at the one you decide on. I've not seen this much rain all winter.'

It rained solidly all that first day, and continued throughout the next. As early as noon on Saturday the RUC had been warned of the prospect of flash flooding and the entire fire service was on the alert as the steady downpour continued to build up. We heard on the radio that all weekend leave in Down, Antrim, and Armagh had been cancelled and volunteers were already assembling in the stations. I thought myself fortunate to have caught the early bus, it seemed as though no more were getting through.

'It's wild,' one of Shelagh's neighbours said coming back up the street. 'The lower road's all awash, I've just seen them turn an Ulsterbus back and they're not letting any more traffic go down that way. It's all being rerouted away from the coast road. I wouldn't go down there for love nor money today.'

Her voice was hard to hear above the drumming of the constant rain. I saw people running past the window, blown like litter across the street. Some clutched useless umbrellas that turned inside out and pulled them along. Even from where I stood by the fire I felt the moisture carried on the wind. I must have been on the other side of the room a good ten feet away from the front door, yet I felt my face become damp before Shelagh closed it.

'Listen Shelagh, suppose this keeps up all weekend? How will I get back? I've to be in work on Monday.'

'Don't worry about that, I can fix you up with a lift. The greengrocer now, let's see, he goes up to the city every day. There'd have to be six foot of water before Davie Finnegan would leave that wee shop of his locked up. Mind you, you'll have to shift early. He leaves just before six every morning but at least you can be sure of getting there. I had a word with a couple of the fishermen the other day and arranged for us to go out in a boat with Big Liam, he's not superstitious about women in boats. Mind you, it won't be superstitions that stop them going out today.'

She stared out of the window hearing the sharp cracks of thunder. I was extremely relieved.

'There won't be anyone out fishing today surely?'

'No,' she said, 'shame isn't it?'

When Shelagh remarked that we could not just sit in all

day, I tensed, expected her to suggest a walk along the flooded coast road to see if there were any boats out that we might be able to join, so I was delighted when she made the suggestion of a sprint down to the wharf for a quick drink at one of the pubs. 'You might meet some of the local characters,' she said.

I stood in front of the fire and watched the steam hiss from my saturated jeans. I had to keep turning so that I would not burn; I had all the rough comfort I needed. Everyone in the bar seemed to be breathless as if they had all rushed in at the same moment. I heard Shelagh ask for two hot bushes for 'medicinal purposes' and an older woman, who I would have placed in her forties, turned around and began to laugh. Shelagh obviously knew her, they chatted for a while and I could overhear bits of the conversation where I stood, a complete stranger in this small, incestuous place.

'We were no sooner out of the Square, just come away from our Thomas's when there was this terrific bolt of lightning and our Aileen said to me, let's get inside Mam, so we ran.'

The woman's daughter nodded, 'That's right we did.'

'Well I thought, we might just as well run in here as go back to the son's,' the woman grinned 'Might as well have a bit of crack. Though God only knows how we're going to walk home again in this.'

I overheard Shelagh ask about a baby. Later I discovered that this woman was Mrs McNaughton, whose son Thomas had become a father for the first time that week. She was the proud grandparent come to gloat.

'Och, he's gorgeous entirely,' she gushed.

'Ah he is too,' the bar maid agreed. 'I was round there only yesterday. Annie's looking well. She told me she had an easy time. She's lucky. My God, I wouldn't want to repeat any of mine. I told her, I'm glad I've had all I'm going to have, that's the wonderful thing about middle age, you're free.'

'You're right there Nelly,' the other woman answered, then all their voices dropped until Shelagh must have said something which made them laugh.

'At any road you could all be here for a spell yet,' Nelly warned.

'Then we might just as well make the best of it,' Mrs McNaughton said, 'give us two glasses of Guinness.'

It was a pleasure to see Nelly pouring porter. Here, I thought, was someone who could handle the stuff. Her expert hands knew exactly how far to tip the glass. I was sure that she would never knock the head off with a knife. She would have hated such sloppy work for she took each pint slowly and carefully, letting the bottom fill up gradually from the even stream. She held the glass in such a way that the drink hit the side exactly how it needed to deaden the impact and allow the black liquid to rise slowly to the top with just a half inch of creamy lather like the frill on a woman's petticoat. I could see that her touch was well appreciated. Shelagh remarked later that some of those people in the bar must have run past both Kierney's and Foggarty's to be out of the rain at that particular public house.

Over at the bar I saw the daughter take off her dripping head scarf. Under it her hair was a type of ginger which I have never seen again. It gave me a shock for I had never seen hair like it before, so bright or indeed so curly. To call it red would fail to describe it accurately – there was no sublety in it, this hair was orange. At first my reaction was to think it was a nylon wig and a stupid-looking one at that, one of the worst of those dreadful things that had become popular in the mid-sixties and were sold all over the country in chain stores as replacements to hats. I thought that she was out of touch. Then as I watched she began to comb through it with her fingers, tugging and pulling in a manner which demonstrated that this was no wig. I thought then that it must have been a severe case of perming and a heavy-handed dose of the dye bottle, but I was wrong there too.

Aileen crossed over to the fire and seeing me for the first time remarked in a friendly manner that her hair went wild in the rain too. As my hair dried it curled up tightly as though I had suffered an electric shock.

'I don't know why I ever had this done,' I grimaced putting my hand up to it. It felt rough and coarse like wire wool against my palm.

Mrs McNaughton had come over with Shelagh and sitting down, could not stop herself from exclaiming in surprise, 'Is that not natural! Do you mean to tell me that you paid good money to have that done to yourself!' and she started to laugh. She tried to control herself, but the joke was so enormous that she could only succeed in spluttering. 'I'm sorry love, it's just that I think it's wild funny that someone would choose to have hair looking like . . . ' She could not finish the sentence for laughing.

Shelagh guffawed, and after that we all did.

'You'll have to excuse my mother,' Aileen grinned. 'But I'd pay good money to have my hair straightened and flattened right out, so I would.'

We were still all laughing when Mrs McNaughton having taken her first mouthful of Guinness said, 'Och you young girls are never satisfied.' Then turning to me she asked if I worked in Belfast.

'Shelagh was telling us that you're only down for the weekend. Shame about the weather. But tell me, isn't it wild up there with all the shootings? I wouldn't go up there for a pension, not nowadays.'

We talked about the village. It was Aileen who told me that I really should try to see the woods at the back before I left and she described them lovingly as only one who knows somewhere from birth can. She said that they were the best bits of the countryside. As she spoke I observed her with interest. She was pale, her skin so white as to be colourless. It looked almost transparent where it stretched tightly over her cheek bones. She was thin, over-thin if anything; her face was fashionably hollow in the right places. She struck me as one of those pale and interesting people who manage to convey their mysterious personality by their silence. She was friendly but not over fond of talking, preferring to listen. I remember that when she ventured an opinion it was clear and decisive. I was intrigued. There was an enigmatic quality about her as though she harboured a great truth, or an awful secret. I would not have placed her as being more than twenty yet there was something aged about her, something which cut across her girlishness and seemed to mock it.

Mrs McNaughton commented on my Liverpool accent and asked where my parents had come from originally. I told them that my father came from Belfast, from the Markets area. Betty became rather excited.

'That's where I'm from originally. What's your father's name? I might know him.'

She screwed up her forehead as she thought. 'Ah I don't. I can't remember anyone by that name'.

It has always been the same; whenever I meet anyone from the same place as my father, they never remember him. I suppose that I have always wanted someone to say, 'Och . . . that feller . . .' and regale me with stories about his youth, stories that for some reason he would never tell us himself. If we pestered him, he made them up. Imaginary stories about places he had never been, about people he had never known. It was as if he dreaded us getting near to the truth. I used to wonder if he ever had a childhood.

'Wouldn't he be much older than Betty if he were still alive?' Shelagh asked.

'Oh yes, he'd be in his seventies now. He left Belfast in the thirties.'

'Let's see,' Betty counted, 'I'm forty-five . . . och, I'd have only been a baby, that's if I was born at all while he was still living there. Aye love, I wouldn't remember him.'

Once when I was playing I peered over my father's shoulder as he wrote out his mass card for All Souls' Day. It was a pure accident. I thought that he was doing the crossword. It was then that I first saw the mysterious secret *names of his dead*. I read the names Margaret and Elisabeth Lynch before he saw me and snatched the card away into his pocket calling for my mother to remove me and give me something useful to do out in the kitchen, muttering about idle minds. Something in his face stopped me asking him any questions. I knew that I had stumbled upon one of his secrets. Years later I discovered the facts about his first marriage. Such things have a way of working themselves out. He believed that he took his knowledge with him to the grave and it was kinder to let him believe this, but I have in my possession the torn brown photograph that my mother could not bear to throw away. My father, younger and stronger than I was ever to know him, pushing his first wife in a wheelchair. On the back, written in his hand, Elisabeth, and the date 1927. A year later she was dead. I learned that he nursed her through the worst of her wasting disease. He had married her knowing that she might die, he must have loved her desperately. I think that it was this knowledge which caused my mother to suffer as he grew harder and more weary of the daily imperfections of real life and the memory of his first wife became a perfect ideal to him. My mother could never forget what none were supposed to know.

'I wonder if you might remember someone called Margaret Lynch?' I asked. 'Maybe they called her Maggie? You see my father was married before, and his wife died but her mother came from Cromac Square too. Maggie Lynch?'

'There was old Mrs Lynch. She was housebound.'

'Did she have children? Did she have a daughter by the name of Elisabeth?'

'She had two girls, no sons at all. Mind you the girls were well grown up: they had their own children who would be the same age as me. I can't remember what they were called. Not Elisabeth, no, not that. I was the only Betty. Come to think of it . . . Old Mrs Flynn used to talk about another daughter, och, but she had died years before. She was an invalid.'

'That's her!' I shouted, excited beyond belief that here at last was confirmation of my father's life. 'That was my father's first wife. Maggie Lynch was his mother in law.'

Shelagh looked amazed. 'You never told me any of this.'

'I never thought it mattered. After all, I never knew them. My father never went back to Belfast, but when Mrs Lynch died he always remembered her and had masses said.'

Aileen looked at her mother. 'You must remember something about Mrs Lynch,' she coaxed, wanting to draw out the information that she sensed was important to me. That's what I remember about her, that there was a genuine kindness in spirit. 'It's a small world,' she said, instantly establishing the only link possible between myself, the outsider, and her mother.

'Old Mrs Lynch used to smoke something terrible, day in, day out. She was always sending us up to the shop to get her a single fag when she had none left. My da, well not only him, but most of the working neighbours, would get her a packet of ten on pay day. She used to sit out on the steps during the hot weather. The B Specials used to come into the street firing their guns in a show of strength. God they were swines. We'd all scatter, pull the blinds; but she couldn't move as fast. She used to yell at them that they ought to show respect. She was a tough one all right. And those same men would be out walking on the twelfth carrying the bloody banner. My da wouldn't let us out the house in case there was trouble. We had all our front windows smashed once and he wouldn't let my brothers go out to find them. "They'll be back tomorrow in their uniforms," he said, and you can't argue with the other end of a pistol now can you?'

Aileen sat quietly by while her mother remembered growing up in the Markets. Suddenly the woman's face changed, she grew brighter and a tone of pride came into her voice. She asked me if I was 'courtin' and smiled broadly when she told me that Aileen was. 'He's a lovely boy,' she said, then, leaning forward and dropping her voice, 'His family's Protestant,' she whispered and straightened up. 'But I've met his mother. She's widowed like myself, but she's a right decent woman. I liked her anyway. There are good Protestants and bad Catholics you know. I wonder what her daddy would have had to say about it. . . . And there's our Bridget, isn't her young man English, isn't that a funny thing now?'

'Och Mam, these things don't matter so much nowadays. It's what they're like as people that counts.'

'Indeed, you're right,' agreed her mother, taking a sip of Guinness. 'You won't make the same mistakes that we made. More people should be able to cross over the barriers. We've put them up amongst ourselves for too long now. Do you know that when I was growing up in Belfast if I'd have brought a Protestant lad home with me I think my daddy would have killed me. It's the men that get all hot under the collar about it . . . we women don't care, as long as they treat you right that's what I say.' She sat back, having resolved the conflict in Northern Ireland. I noticed that Aileen blushed and I thought she was being demure, but now I think her reasons were otherwise.

'Bloody men, I can't see the point in them myself,' Shelagh said, 'not unless you want gangs of kids. I'm happy enough being my own woman, earning my own living. I wouldn't let any man pay for my way in the world.'

Aileen was silent, but Betty laughed.

'Ah you'll change, you've plenty of time to make your ma a grandmother; you'll make us all grannies yet, see if I'm not right.'

That evening when Shelagh and I were sitting round the fire in her house I asked her about Aileen. I had been intrigued by her quiet manner.

'Oh I often see her and her sister Bridget about the village. They're very close, very good friends you don't often find one without the other. She's the eldest. Bridget must be two years younger, but she's the one with all the schemes and plans. Would you believe but when that child was only seven she arranged for one of the fishermen to row her and Aileen around to the other side of the bay – Bridget thought that was where America was and she had told Aileen that they were emigrating! They turned up with their dolls and a packet of sweets between them for the journey and stood crying saying that they wanted to go home, and the poor old sod who was giving them a ride in his boat didn't know what was the matter with them. Eventually he got the story from them and didn't he laugh, telling them that America was much further away. The next week Bridget was back wanting to hire a boat because she had worked out that she could row herself to America if Aileen would take over when she got tired as it was so much further away than she'd first planned. Big Liam told me that.' Shelagh smiled.

'But it was funny how I got to know Aileen. I'd seen her around but I'd never spoken to her; you know how you can sometimes know people by sight but not to talk to? I used to see her and her sister down on the shore a lot talking to the fishermen. No one in the family earns their living by the sea, funny that isn't it? Those who don't work on the sea can usually enjoy it more. But she was rather embarrassed by our first meeting, in fact she called round to apologise the next day.'

'Why? What happened?'

'It was between three and four in the morning. I was woken up by the sound of something moving about in my garden. I lay awake listening trying to convince myself that it was an animal, a badger or a stoat that had wandered in from the woods. But I heard it coughing. I hoped that it was one of the lads that were down from Belfast. I'd seen some just a few days before camping in the woods. I thought that I could handle that quite easily if it turned out to be some youngster with too much drink taken who had got himself lost. But then it struck me that it could just as easily be a burglar and I felt frightened. I hadn't moved in that long to be drawing attention to myself by being the first person ever to be burgled here. I know that sounds stupid but all manner of notions were rushing through my head. I was a bit scared by now, I'll be honest. Then I began thinking that it might be a local man who had taken exception to me, you know, a woman alone and all that. I started wondering if someone had turned up to show me that I needed a man and maybe whoever it was had spent all night drinking, brooding about it, and was out there in the garden waiting for his chance. My mind was rioting by now so there was no point pretending to lay calmly in my bed. I got up and put my gardening boots on. Great strong soles they have, thinking I'd kick the living daylights out of whoever it was if they'd thought to come frightening me. I crept downstairs. Everything was still. I looked at the clock, it was not four. That's some hour to be up and about! I took my overcoat down from behind the door and went over to peer through the window.

'It was a lovely night. Bright with the moon just a sliver

off full. I could make out the trees at the edge of the lesser
woods. The sky was clear and starry, I recognised the
Plough high up to the west . . . in the name of God! star
watching at that time of night . . . then something caught
my eye. There was someone in my garden. I hadn't
imagined it! I stood behind the curtain hardly daring to
breathe and whoever it was had gone very still as though
they knew they were being watched. My palms were
sweating, I edged over to the stand and took a great stick
of blackthorn that I keep for blackberrying; by God, I
meant to take the head off them! Then I saw something
reflecting the moon. It was the girl's hair. It looked like
gold. She stepped forward, horribly visible. Paler than
usual she seemed to have a terrible brilliance about her. It
gave me quite a turn, but once I'd seen who it was I was
no longer scared and I opened the door quickly to go out
to her. Suddenly she lurched over and vomited into that
laurel bush.' Shelagh's eyes rolled towards the wall to
indicate the exact spot as if she could see the bush clearly
through it. 'I was angry at that because I thought she
must have been drinking to get herself into such a state,
turning up and frightening the wits out of me; I thought
that she might faint . . . I'd never heard retching and
moaning like it . . . I raced towards her to give her a hand.
God, she looked like she really was in a bad way. I'd only
once got that bad after a works party when I still lived in
Belfast. Two people had to bring me home in a taxi and I
swore never again. But would you believe that the girl
wasn't drunk? In fact I'd swear to her not having a drop
inside. She was as sober as I was only a deal more
frightened. I'd never seen anything like the look in her
eyes, it was as if she'd seen Hell. She was trembling all
over but she wouldn't come inside; all she'd say was that
she had a row with her mother. It's odd but then stranger
things do happen; who knows what goes on. Still, there's
been no lasting effects has there? You've seen her and

Betty together, they seem to get along fine now. Aileen told me that she'd come out for a walk to clear her head; she was more thoughtful than usual and then she turned and went in the direction of the shore. I remember that her feet were all covered in clay so she must have been that way already, there's a couple of very loamy fields just before the shore, if you walk across them you all but sink.'

'What did you do?'

'I just stood in my garden for a while looking at the stars. There was a strange smell, I thought it was like petrol. Then I went back indoors.'

'Tell me about her family,' I asked, intrigued still further by the image of Aileen alone at the shore in the dark.

'Was there any reason for thinking that there might have been a row?'

'Not really. They always seemed a happy enough family to me. I never told anyone about that night. Aileen came to apologise the next day and asked me not to mention it, she said that she didn't want her mother getting upset again. I asked around a bit. I was curious about her. My next-door neighbours told me later that her elder brother's in the 'Kesh. Not Thomas, he's the one whose wife's just had the baby, no, there's another brother a year younger than him; Dominic. He was put in detention when he was sixteen and later transferred.'

'Why, what had he done?'

'Och, it seems a few years before there was a lot of trouble here. A student teacher down from college was recruiting from the pupils up at Saint Malachy's. There was an explosion up at the RUC station; one of the men was injured. A policeman,' Shelagh added seeing my confusion. 'They rounded up five youths, not one of them over the age of sixteen and they were all attending Saint Malachy's. Dominic was among them. They got eight years each. Bloody stiff. The RUC uncovered several guns that were hidden in the wood that same week and they tried to pin possession on the lads but it didn't stick. Mr McNaughton was one of the old-style patriots. It broke his heart when his son was taken. He held himself responsible for filling the boy up with romantic notions of Ireland.

'I never knew him, he died when Dominic was still inside. They wouldn't let the son out to attend his father's funeral. People here were really angry at that. There was a demonstration outside the RUC station. The whole thing was bloody ironic though; old Mr McNaughton believed that education was the answer to Northern Ireland's ills. He felt that if enough people were educated they would be able to see the situation in a fairer light and the issues would be resolved through the ballot box. Thomas takes after his father in all that; he was the golden boy. At the time all this was going on he must have still been at Queen's. It's sad though that the old feller put all his trust in education and it was up at a school that the other son was learning about petrol bombs. Betty has a much harder line – I've talked to her occasionally about it, she said to me once that she thought her husband must have been naïve because he really seemed to think that privilege could be easily given up. Privilege! God knows the advantages the one side have here are bloody meagre anyway. I suppose because she grew up in the city it was harder for her to have any romantic notions. Did your father ever talk about it?'

'Sometimes. He told me once that he'd had to crawl along the pavement because the police were firing on a crowd of Saint Patrick's night revellers. He didn't say much about his life, only that he couldn't get a job and they still had notices up in shop windows saying Catholics needn't apply.'

'Makes me want to bloody spit. You can't blame some

youngster for taking it into their head to strike a blow back. I can't.'

She was silent for a while. Outside the rain was still coming down, running in the gutters like swift flowing streams.

'The ballot's been too well rigged in Ulster,' she said finally.

'Does Aileen go to see her brother?'

'Dominic? He requested no more visits because of all the searches he had to go through each time, and also he said he didn't enjoy seeing what it was doing to his mother. That's what I heard anyway.'

When the rain did stop it was late on Sunday evening and we had spent an entire weekend listening to it drumming against the slates, watching it drip from the leaves of the laurel bush. Apart from the couple of hours at the pub on Saturday we did not venture out but remained as if withstanding a siege, indoors. I don't think that I had ever seen such furious rain. Even those people I glimpsed through the window walked with their heads bent as if pushed down by the force of it falling constantly. The tide was at its highest point before flooding and only the foolhardy ventured outdoors. I did not manage to see the woods, which was a disappointment especially after Aileen described them. She made them sound as being amongst the best places on earth. In fact I'm sure that's how she put it.

'You know in the time I've been here I feel as though they're my own private woods too. That's how the local people feel, after all they have grown up with them and they feel rightly that they belong to them. And they really are quite magical. I've seen them in winter when they are black shadowed and bare and I've caught the tail end of their autumn when everything is copper and there's such a smell of burning leaves. The best time of all is when the bluebells are up in the spring, in summer there are just too many people about. Then the woods are no longer private and that's really where their charm lies.'

'Isn't the fuschia beautiful then?'

'I don't know, sometimes when I see fuschia now I think the heavy heads are too like blood drops,' and she shrugged as if trying to shake something off.

Although the rain was over by Monday, Shelagh had 'fixed it up' too well for me with Davie Finnegan's wife so that any attempt to travel up on the seven-thirty bus would have looked ungrateful. The greengrocer thumped on the door at six o'clock, precise and businesslike.

'Are you right then girl?' he asked. 'If you sit up at the front, just mind those crates don't slip as you're getting in. I've to make a detour along the coast road – I said I'd leave off a parcel one of the Neason sisters is sending the other. I think she's knitted her another cardigan,' he grinned, feeling the brown paper packet that was lying on the seat. 'How many cardigans do you need I ask you; that's the fourth she's sent since winter.'

He picked it up carefully and stowed it along the dashboard. 'I'll just leave it sitting on her door step, she'll find it when she takes in the milk. If I knock her up now, she'll start talking and I'll not see Belfast in daylight. I can give her a knock when I'm coming home this evening to see if she wants to return anything to her sister. She usually does the socks – the other one can't turn heels.'

I climbed into the van. As far as the eye could see there were cabbages stacked up to the roof, hundreds of them, leafy, green and dark, dropping leaves through the open slats of the crates which lurched terrifyingly every time he turned a corner or came to a halt. After a while I noticed that everything had the same muddy earthy smell of soil and vegetation.

'Wild weather we've been having,' he commented as the

van rolled down the empty street leading out of the village.

'The wife told me that you were just staying the weekend. She was talking to Shelagh the other day. I hear you were talking to Betty McNaughton. Isn't it wild about her son? Terrible pity that, terrible. Ah, they were wild times, wild times indeed.'

'That was a few years back wasn't it?' said I, feigning innocence. 'It must have been before Shelagh lived here.'

'Aye, that's right. It was all before her time.'

'Mrs McNaughton's son is in Long Kesh isn't he?'

'Oh dear God, I only wish he was.'

'What do you mean?'

'He's on the run. He's been out the 'Kesh the last two years, but the family haven't seen him. God alone knows what he's up to. I blame that young student feller, the one that came here teaching, for putting all sorts of ideas into their heads. This place suffered.' He drew air in between his teeth slowly. They were massive teeth, each one stood a little apart as if testing their strength without the others. We called it 'being gat spaced'. They were heavily stained with tobacco, yet I do not remember him smoking all the way up in the van. His voice sounded almost contemptuous when he spoke again.

'Five of its sons behind bars. Explosions. Do you know that the warehouses along the front were blown up? They were bombed twice. They'd just rebuilt the main storage areas and got them back in use and they went up again the next week.'

'Who did it, and why should they want to?'

'Och, they said that it was someone with a private grudge coming down from the city. Like, it never bothered us Henry being a Protestant. He's lived here all his life and his father before him. He's as much right to inherit his father's business as the next man. But some people they're twisted. One side is as bad as the other to my way of thinking. This place was being torn apart. After that student and two others blew themselves up in the woods we'd hoped that it would all quieten down. It was a bloody stupid business altogether. He'd a car loaded with gelignite – him and two others. They were going to drive over to Springhill and destroy the big house. Can you see any point in that? I know it was built by Ulster settlers but it's a bit late now isn't it? They've settled. It's one of the few historic buildings we've got and there's no Lord of the Manor collecting taxes now. Jesus! It's National Trust. I take my kids there for picnics. Picnics!' He shook his head in disgust.

'What happened?'

'They were taking the car through the lower woods at night when they must have hit something on the road. The whole lot went up.'

'How do you know that's where they were going?'

'There were others involved. They were to meet along the Moneymore road. They never turned up. Somehow the story got known that the big house had been targeted.'

From the van's high seat I looked down on the deep puddles that lay across the road. Everywhere could be seen the damage caused by the heavy rains. Newly ploughed fields had turned into lakes of mud. I saw half buried farm machinery, broken railings. My eyes took in the devastation while Davie Finnegan speculated on the going rate for vegetables.

'There'll be that much stock wiped out, I dare say there won't be any early produce. It's a rough life all right.'

We looped back from the coast into the outskirts of the village and he put his foot down hard as we approached the RUC station. 'Did Shelagh tell you that when Betty's husband died they wouldn't let her son out to attend the funeral? His own father! God, that made me bloody mad.' Again there was the sucking in of air.

'People were disgusted. A gang went up to that station,' he looked at it in his rear mirror with no particular expression as it grew smaller surrounded in its barbed wire cage.

'Aye, they went up in a gang and all the windows got smashed. They must have used wire cutters to get in . . . there were no arrests. It was old schoolmates of Dominic's settling a score. When they buried the student up in Milltown it was on the news. They gave him full military honours, the Tricolour draped over the coffin. When the cortege got near the gates of the cemetary four masked IRA men appeared and flanked the pallbearers, and there was a column of teenagers, schoolkids mostly, maybe twenty or thirty of them. They came forward through the crowd, I suppose someone must have given a signal because thay all put on black berets and marched in strict formation behind the coffin just as it entered the cemetery. They stood to attention while shots were fired over the grave. When it was seen on the evening news some people round here thought that they recognised the sisters in with the black-bereted column following the coffin. Betty was worried sick. Her own husband only buried and her not yet over that shock, to be told that her kids might have been on UTV looking for all the world as if they'd enlisted. I never saw it myself but there are some folk round here who'll swear that it was the sisters. All I can say is that if it was them, then it was just an act to ease the blow they had suffered by Dominic's absence at their father's funeral. They probably thought that they would at least step into his place for your man's funeral as the authorities had not seen fit to release him for their father's.

'What's that story about cutting off the hydra's head? Don't more spring up? I reckon that's what they were showing the authorities. Mess about with their brother and they would be there to take his place. But it was only a gesture, there's none of them at all like Dominic. Look at Thomas. He's up teaching at the school now.'

I had plenty to think about on the journey back. The various bits of information that I had heard about Aileen did not at all fit in with the quiet woman I had met the day before. There was something still missing.

I did not see Aileen again although I heard news. I heard for instance that both the McNaughton girls had married with the boys their mother had so proudly spoken of that day in the pub. I heard that Aileen had a child and lived outside the village and that Bridget went to live with the English man in Dublin where his company had moved. Shelagh remarked once that it was strange to see Aileen walking by the shore road pushing a pram, knowing that Bridget would not be waiting for her around the corner.

'Even in the short time that I'd seen them I've grown used to the sight of them always going about together. If I ran into one I usually knew that the other could not be that far off.'

Years later a newspaper heading caught my eye. BOMB ATTACK SISTERS IMPRISONED. I read down. . . . 'Two sisters were charged in Crumlin Road this morning for their involvement in an arson attack on a furniture shop.' My eye skimmed the column. The attack had taken place in 1974 but the sisters who, according to the newspaper, had married since and both had families, were only being charged now, six years after the attack took place. Somehow they had managed to evade capture. I read on; the attack was carried out in a small town in the same county and not too far from where Shelagh lived.

I was living in England by this time and I suppose that I read the news with a feeling of local interest more than anything else, until I felt my stomach lurch. In just a few brief sentences the description of the identikit pictures which had appeared on Ulster TV brought the whole affair right onto my doorstep. This must be Aileen McNaughton, she would have a different name through her marriage, and this other woman, Bridget Wallis, must be her sister, it was surely them. That orange hair of Aileen's had betrayed them. She would have been painfully obvious to anyone who knew her, anyone who was able to put the facts together. I felt numb. Shelagh had no telephone or I would have cast caution to the wind and rung her at once. Instead I had to write for confirmation. Shelagh replied immediately that it was the McNaughton sisters.

It was a few months after the news of their arrest that I was next in Belfast. I met up with Shelagh in the middle of the day.

'Do you remember me telling you how I first met Aileen, how strange it was? I seem to remember that about that time there was news of an arson attack on a furniture shop in one of the small towns. But as it wasn't in the village it did not have that much local interest, considering what everyone had gone through. I certainly never associated the two things. Aileen turning up like that and the report. I remember that the news story was vague. An incendiary device was thrown in through a window that had been smashed with a brick. Eye witnesses saw two movements, very well co-ordinated, as if the same person had performed them simultaneously. I can imagine that the sisters were at first euphoric, striking a blow; but things went very badly wrong. There was a flat over the shop and two people were burned to death.

'After their arrest when Mrs McNaughton had visited them separately, she said that both girls told her they knew nothing about the flat. They both swore that the first they realised there was someone living above the shop was when they heard the cries for help. I believe that. I don't think either of them intended such violence.'

'What age were they then?'

'Fifteen and seventeen, and you know the rest.'

'What do you mean?'

'I mean their marriages; to an English man and a Protestant. It couldn't be more obvious that they were trying to cut themselves off from the Provies. They made it seem as if they had little interest in politics. They lay low, they had kids. Aileen's got two now you know. I think they must have been horrified by the violence of the attack. Sick with it. After all they had killed civilians not soldiers. It stunned them out of all further activity. God, they were only a couple of kids. To have that on their consciences. . . .

'They must have made sure that they never spoke about anything in front of their husbands that might brand them as having once been politically involved. Aileen's husband was awful: he turned up outside Mrs McNaughton's, shouting and screaming about Catholics being liars, being the worst imaginable things – it was as if he could no longer imagine the Aileen he had known. He spat out the foulest names, called her a bitch, a whore, said she was like an animal that should be fucked on all fours . . . he ranted about Catholics always being hot for it, said that he'd given her two kids already but she wanted more . . . it was awful, awful, I can't repeat it. . . . Thomas had to come down to make him go away. He'll fill those kids up with hate if he ever tells them about their mother. He obviously thought he'd done his bit for world development by marrying a Catholic. He had no right to say all that filth to Mrs McNaughton; but the other one, oh he was very calm, restrained. Embarrassed almost that he was returning to England. He said that his child could not possibly have any contact with them. He hoped Mrs McNaughton would understand. Understand! I think he was the worst; he must have made her feel that she was all those things he didn't like to say; his silence was damning. She's lost three grandchildren as well as two daughters. You should see her, she aged overnight from when they were first arrested.

'The entire village is horrified, no one thought that they could be guilty at first, but lately, bits and pieces of news are all put together. Mary, one of Aileen's neighbours, saw her being arrested, she was looking out the window when the RUC drew up. Aileen was hanging out washing in the back garden and the men came down the path. Mary ran around the side of the house. She said that they took hold of Aileen from behind and held her so that she couldn't move while the baby was crawling about her feet. Mary ran at them screaming that it was a mistake, she told them Aileen's name and shouted that they had the wrong person . . . but she said that the look on Aileen's face was strange; she was shaking her head and making no fuss, resigned to her arrest. Mary thought that it was almost with a sense of relief that she let them lead her away. I remember seeing a statement that the Provies issued, not in relation to this affair but to another . . . something to the effect that everything possible is always done to avoid civilian casualties but that no war can be fought without them. For me, those sisters are casualties.'

Three or four months after my visit to Belfast the sisters' case finally came up. I saw the short paragraph in the newspaper. It was on an inside page, quite easy to miss. Both sisters had been found guilty of manslaughter and given sentences of fifteen years each. Neither of the women's husbands nor any of their husbands' families attended the trial.

THE MOTHER RIGHT

Andrea Freud Lowenstein

Gwendolyn, speaking

It was not from going to them and ask for help all this happen, my Anthony. The welfare yes, because I must, but never have I ask a crumb more than what they fix among theyself to give we. Helen downstair, she run to them each time she need some little nothing and leave she kids in the house for mischief but you know I not about to leave you alone my Anthony, and how I to take three kids on that bus now? Just to go see these people the way they look at you like you dirt, you seen it Anthony, the times you been with me. And that bus, sometime it will not stop at the same place where it have stop before and you know it hard for me to tell the driver where. The way my leg can get to shake sometime on the way from the seat where he sit and then I get afraid, what if I should fall flat down on my face in the aisle, then the ugliness I should see looking up in the people face, how they all look away quick like they don' see nothing or else gather all close to peer like wolves at the carrion. You have seen it, Anthony, I know you have seen.

The one they send me, she who is we colour but who know nothing of we, she say, 'Talk, Gwendolyn, talk, get it off your chest.' But who is there to talk to but you, my son? If she think I talk to she, the woman crazy, so she can go make a report for they to take you from me.

Julius, he still a baby, too young to understand. And you sister, she don' listen, she always want to go play, she is hard, not soft like you, my son, she is born as we say backhome well known. With she it always no no, let me do it myself. While you, my son, you still need I to button you, to tie the shoes, and is you warm body, you and Julius on the other side that keep me still warm and human. Because without no touch at all I turn to stone, and what do a lady know of that who they have already taken and turn to stone, like theyself, or to a piece of soap without no substance that melt in the water if you touch she. No, it is you alone who can understand, Anthony. Because you are smart, and I know it even if this teacher of you she do not.

'Too many absent,' she mark down on this card of their, and 'Will not speak up in class.' And call me in one time to tell me it *I* have hold you back. Who they think taught you read and write before you even pass through the door of their so call school, and your sister too? They think maybe you grab it out the air? 'Take him to the library,' she have the nerve to tell me when we go there every week and have read every book they got for kids on they shelf. And even Shakespeare, from the play you all three name after, the one I read before my school leaving. And what do she know about the book we make together, we four?

Slow they write down on their paper, slow, but you and I we know what they writing for true. Only their ignorance, big as the sea. For who is it they see when they see you? A child dark as these others, the hopeless ones, the black they got here in this country of hatefulness that speak like dumb animal that bang they head in they own dirt like a proud tiger in a cage until they dim they own understanding. A dark one they see, a small and quiet one. And what can I do if you chose to sit apart, son, to hold your peace when that vulture she call your name to read and in her voice she say slow, slow?

And why should I go to such as she for help? It is not of

my doing, son, the time I lose my breath waiting for three hour on they line with all of you crying cause you hungry and you wet. If they so so concern why they don' provide us some chairs to sit and wait for they little bit of a check, instead of all the thing they have bring down on my weary head after that one time?

One Black lady spy of my own each Friday at four, to pass she finger over the kitchen table and poke her feet at the floor, a gift like that I could well live without, hmm, Anthony? One white college boy to take you to the ball game and play with you. I seen it how he drive that car of he, screech it around the corners, if he should let harm come to you then I tell you they will see my meekness. Then they will see the lion roar under the tame cat they think they got in Gwendolyn Prophet.

If you will get hurt in the car, Anthony? How am I to know? You think it God he ownself you see here and not your mother? Only I know cars like that, sometime they crash, hmm? And Cleo, one for she too, that white lady they send me the first time from the welfare. Such a big important lady for only a little girl, Anthony. 'Because I fell in love with her the first day I met her,' remember how she tell it? And what right do she have, that one, with her barren flank the color of milk soured to fall in love with someone child?

Let her go and make she own, not take mine and spell her so she cling to she hand. Anthony, I ever tell you of the catbird? That a bird that come and steal other people egg out the nest when they not looking. But me, I am looking.

Adele, writing
When I brought Cleo home today, her mother still wouldn't speak to me, or even look at me. At first she wouldn't even look at Cleo either, as if I'd contaminated her, and of course the other two were already screaming. All that screaming, in that awful pandemonium of an

apartment, as if a tornado had just swept through it. Although Cleo is always remarkably well dressed and immaculate.

After a minute Gwen did speak to Cleo, but with such venom! 'So! You are so busy out having a good time with your lady you miss the ice cream and now there is no more left.' Then Cleo started screaming too, and got down on the floor in a tantrum. God, I hate to see her like that. With me she's always so – proud is a grownup word for a six-year-old, but it's one of the right ones for her.

Locked up or defended are right too, even when she wants something badly, or is excited about something. Like at the aquarium today with that wave machine. Funny, I found it boring compared to the fish and all the live things, but she loved to press the button and see the electric blue lines of wave reverse themselves and start to swing around the other way, she couldn't stop doing it, and her eyes were all lit up. I think what she loved so much was having that much control, unlike at home.

Or when we went to the science museum last week, and the girl held out the skunk and asked who wanted to stroke it. Cleo's eyes blazed the way they do, with that passion of wanting, but she wouldn't volunteer, only nodded very sedately when I asked her, then, when she had passed her hand over the fur, letting a tiny smile escape. 'He feels soft!' And then, sort of diffidently, 'My Mommy says never touch an animal. She says watch out for Cindy's cat it could claw you and then it might get infected and your arm drop off.' She was trying it out on me, conversationally. At first I just said, 'This skunk is very safe, they wouldn't let him hurt anyone,' not wanting to challenge Mommy on the cat business. But then I did, I couldn't bear it. I said, 'Your arm won't fall off from a cat scratch, Cleo, I think what your mother meant was just be careful.' She put her thumb in her mouth and stared at me. Now I know why she shrinks against me whenever we pass a dog in the street.

But she doesn't swallow it whole, the poison, the fear. She wanted to pet the skunk, and she did. I think it was that which grabbed me on my first visit, after the welfare office contacted me and asked me to come and make a recommendation. They'd already had someone check the City Hospital, where aparently Cleo and Gwen both have records because of recurring asthma, and with the school, where the oldest, Anthony, is repeating the second grade because of poor attendance and childish behaviour. I don't like to recommend foster care except for in extreme cases, but I have to admit I had my doubts the first time I walked into that amazing clutter to find Gwen sitting in a little cleared-off place on the couch among the old newspapers and torn books and papers and broken plates and ruined toys, clutching both screaming boys to her, and trembling so much she could hardly speak. No one had told her anything about possible removal of the kids, so it couldn't have been that. And there was this little girl, down on the floor, screaming and kicking and shouting, 'No! No!' When Gwen attempted to gather her up too she stopped just long enough to tell her mother, in that strangely adult little voice, 'Leave me alone.'

That was when I wanted her for myself, not for one of the sweet nineteen-year-old college girl big-sisters, who would show her around their dorm room and try to hug her like the teddy bears they only recently outgrew, secretly wishing that she was cuter and more cuddly, more like the other little girls we usually have for them, who are thankful but sneaky. 'Love her, encourage her, don't leave any money around – ' that's my usual rap for the new big sisters. But Cleo would never steal, any more than Gwen would, and even at six no one could call her cute – more like beautiful, with her ebony skin, those dark knowing eyes, her high cheekbones, and her tallness, which makes her look much older than she is., She looks exactly like Gwen, really, as if she'd hatched right out of her with no father involved at all. Which is what they used to say about me and my mother, though I was never able to say no to her like that, let alone tell her to leave me alone. Gwen would be a beautiful woman too, if she ever smiled or relaxed. The two boys are lighter skinned, softer, fuller in the face.

Right from the beginning Cleo felt at home at my place. She already reads really well, God knows how, since she goes to one of the most racist schools in town, and her teacher told me she didn't expect much from her, after all she came from 'one of those project families, and foreign too.' But when I asked her to read to me she said no, she'd rather read to herself. Then she sat down in the big chair with her book, and after a while said, almost meditatively, 'I like it when there's no noise.'

I like it when there's no noise too, I have to remind myself that after she's left. Sometimes I ring Nicki and ask her to repeat back to me what I've said so many times to her. There are other ways to mother. I need my space. I chose to be alone. I chose, I chose. Now that I'm thirty-five it's almost like choosing every minute. And when Cleo is with me and I see her so very tentatively unfolding the petals of her selfhood under my tending – sometimes I'm eaten up with the waste of it. Because I could be a good mother, I know I could. I'd be so different from mine – or from hers. I would never swallow her whole and make her forget who was her and who was me. I'd love her clearly and separately, and let her grow up intact. I have this secret fantasy that Gwen's paranoia will escalate even more and we'll be forced to act. I'm sure they'd let me have her, I'm the adult who knows her best, I don't think Gwen has any family in this country, and they're not going to put kids that age on a plane for Jamaica. She could have my study for her bedroom and the schools around here are much better than the one she goes to now.

Gwendolyn, speaking

You stick with me, Anthony, now you stick here tight to my side and hold me here so you will not get lost in the big store. And you, Julius, stop that screaming right now, is it you want the white ladies to come and take you both away? Like they have take little Larry downstair, you see he is gone now, hmm? Why for? For because his mother leave them kids all by themself one too many time to go and make the goat with some ram or other, that why.

I tell you, Julius, if you keep up that noise they come and take you with not so much as by your leave. Why? Because it give them pleasure, that why. Look now, Anthony, pork chop $1.90 a pound and she have the nerve to talk to me about nutrition planning. How come so many hot dog and do I know what is a balanced meal. And then turn and give me $40.37 to feed three children in this God forsake city. At least backhome if you hungry they will not leave you to starve, here you can die and who notice, hmm? Like the time the stove quit and they din' send no one until three weeks pass. They din' worry bout no balance meal then. Julius, let go that, baby, don't you know what it do it poison little boy finger if they put it in they mouth.

Milk and margarine yes, and beans, look here how they do Anthony, on this cheese. They way they sit it in the carton the rot side away you cannot see until you open him up. Always try and take what little you got. Come now, or we be late for Cleo and you know what happen to little girl when she cannot get in the house? No, not the white lady, Anthony, though maybe you right, she like to steal she a little girl too. No, I mean the child molester, something I never heard of till I come to this great country. A special they got here, to grab little girl up. I see it every day, in the newspaper. Yes they do, they got some for little boy too, that why I tell you don't talk to no one. Yes, I know you don' talk, I know it Anthony. Yes, I told you I give you a note for tomorrow. How she expect me to do my shopping without no one to help, she think I got four hand maybe? You are my big smart man, Anthony, how I do it without you?

Look here boys, we have something over, we can buy a pencil sharpener so we sharpen the pencil, home. And see this pink colour one. And when we get home if you all good and quiet and stop this screaming we will do some more pages on our book, hmm? Yes, Anthony and Julius and Cleo and Gwendolyn and the terrible, wonderful monster. Yes, you shall make a picture on your page with this new pink one and I shall write it down, whatever you say, isn't how we do always, son? And don' show it to no one, don' tell no one. Let they think we slow, this is for we, not they.

Adele, writing
Today I took Cleo to the rainbow workshop to do some painting. At first she just stood there with her thumb in her mouth, watching. I had to bite my tongue not to push, not to tell her again that it was OK to get dirty, that she had the smock on. God, I can still hear my mother now. 'What's the matter with you? Don't stick so close to me all the time! Don't let them push you around, push back! For God's sakes, get your hands dirty, it's not the end of the world.' So I managed to shut up, and finally, finally, when she was ready, she ventured in, carefully putting some black paint on her brush. such deliberation, such precision, and as it turned out, her painting stood out from all of them, it was as if she'd been drawing and painting for years, although I'm sure this was her first time. It was of three small figures, in black, and a much larger one in red. She gave all the smaller ones features and hands and eyes, and the one that was the girl, you could tell from the braids, was the most articulated of all, with five fingers on each hand and a sombre expression –

really amazing work for a six-year-old. The larger figure didn't have any of that, it sort of hovered amorphously on the paper, floating somewhere up in the air. 'Is that a ghost?' asked the teacher, some art therapist type from Bryrdale who was of course fascinated by Cleo. She just shook her head, having clearly decided the woman wasn't worth communicating with. I didn't push her to, figured it was up to her. I was feeling sort of proud and possessive, as if she'd been mine. Maybe all the talking and reading I've done with her have had an effect. When we got to my place she clearly identified each figure for me. 'That's Anthony. See his glasses. That's Julius. He's littlest. That one is me. And that's my Mama.'

I'd hoped she'd leave the painting at my house – I confess I even asked for it, but she looked absolutely stricken, then shook her head, staring at me fearfully. I told her maybe if she came to spend the night at my house next weekend we could make some more pictures. I've been wanting to have her overnight for a while, but have been reluctant to ask because of Gwen. I'd thought a lot about it, and finally decided that although part of Gwen's resentment of me is about my relationship with Cleo, part must be an envy of my freedom. She never has any time to herself without kids, I know she's much too paranoid to leave them with a babysitter. So I'd decided to offer to take all three of them overnight next Saturday, to really give her a break.

As soon as we got there, the boys started to scream. I wonder what Gwen tells them, that I'll kill them? They can't possibly scream like that all day, it's just not possible. I'd think it had to do with my being white, but Elaine, who is Gwen's therapist, or tries to be anyway, is Black, and she reports the same thing. Anyway, as soon as she was in the door, Cleo raced up to her mother. I've never seen the two of them touch, even though Gwen is always intertwined with the boys, but Cleo held out the picture, her eyes flashing. 'For the book!' she said, in that tone of subdued excitement.

Gwen looked at me, then glared at her as if she'd just killed someone, and said, 'What book I don't know what you talking about you stupid girl.' Then she dropped Cleo's painting on the floor, in immediate reach of Julius. He didn't take the bait at first, until she said, in a flat, eerie voice. 'See the pretty picture your sister made, Julius?' I asked her if she didn't want to put it somewhere where he couldn't reach it, but she silenced me with that voice like a slap. 'H'it's OK. Never mind.' Of course by the time I left Julius had torn the picture in two and Cleo was down on the floor absolutely convulsed, screaming and kicking. Gwen came the closest I've ever seen her to smiling. 'She is stubborn as a billy goat,' she told me. 'You see she is getting spoil, with all of these outings.'

It was definitely not the greatest timing, but I went ahead and asked her about Saturday. It seemed even more urgent, somehow, watching Cleo like that, and I guess I thought she might hear even though she didn't let on, and know I was fighting for her. I said I'd like to take either Cleo alone or all three of them if that would give her a break.

'A break,' she said, in that flat mocking voice, as if she didn't know what I meant, or as if it was the stupidest idea she'd ever heard. I've never done so badly with any of the mothers, never! Finally she said, 'Not my boys. But you can take Cleopatra if she want to go.' She pointed to my girl who was still, though a little more weakly, crying and kicking on the floor. I went up to her to try and say goodbye, but she didn't even let me near her. I left feeling like I'd been kicked, not in the hand, where her little foot got me, but in the heart. I was almost in tears in the car wanting so badly just to take her away. Maybe I'll get to next weekend, at least for one night, although probably Gwen will end up forbidding it. I know it could be important to Cleo, though, all the literature says so. To have just one person who holds out something else – it can make all the difference.

Gwendolyn, speaking

Your sister want to go live with the white lady you hear that Anthony? She too good for we now, she don' need we no more. What we do? We let she go with the lady, your sister. I will not stop she. If so, I know what happen next. This white lady go tell them I not co-operating. You think I need someone to tell me what happen next?

No Anthony, stop that now. Mama will not let them take you nowhere. Never mind they fool letter from the school. Now perhaps they gon try and say it my fault you vomit in the morning. Or send he even if he sick. Let the waste they got here in this project send their kid to school with fever without no boot in this killing weather. You seen yourself how Helen downstair do now they already give her Larry back. That one don' deserve no kid but she they give back to and it is I get all these letter, from the school, the welfare, all these God forsake people. Listen now, Julius waking up, we three go and pick up the wash out the dryer. Stop the screaming, baby. Mama sing to you. Soft so no one hear but we. Come on now, Anthony, close the door hard or someone get in when we gone. It better be dry good, cause I got no more quarter. If they wet we have to wear it wet. There Anthony mine, help me fold. Good, now we go and work on the book. Anthony and Julius and Gwendolyn in the land of the terrible wonderful monster. I know I din' say Cleo, son. I know Cleo still at school. My memory not all the way gone yet. She want to go with that catbird lady so bad let her go. We cannot stop her, we. There, now we on our way home, work on we book.

Adele, writing

I've been missing Linda a lot lately. Maybe I'm afraid to let the missing go. I guess even that missing has been company of a kind, a way of not finishing all the way. When that ends, there's emptiness. Of course there's Nicki and Sam, I've got good friends, but it doesn't seem to touch the lack of deep blood connection, of family.

The phone just rang. I can't believe it. This little voice. 'I want to come.' No greeting, no nothing. Just, 'I want to come Saturday,' to the background of the most tremendous screaming. It took me a few seconds to figure it all out. Then I told her how glad I was. I asked to speak to her mother, but Cleo said, 'She said to tell you she's not home. She said I have to call you my ownself. Anthony helped me dial.' After we hung up, I cried. I want her visit to be special, to be something she'll always remember. And who knows what could happen, really, if she likes staying over. Gwen seems to be doing worse and worse every day.

As a child I used to be so terribly homesick whenever I left her. The big H, mother. I hope Cleo won't be homesick. But if she is, I'll hold her, I'll comfort her.

Gwendolyn, speaking

Go then, Cleopatra, go to she. I told you you can decide and you have decide. Don't talk to me now no more. All of that over now, you got your white lady, talk to she, show she your picture. Read to she. You told me how she like to hear you read. Don't cry and act up now. You make your choice.

Adele, writing

The wheezing started at about six. She'd been very quiet all afternoon, with her thumb in her mouth. Didn't want to read, didn't want to paint, didn't want to talk. Everything I asked her she just shook her head no. Her body looked different than I'd ever seen it, too. Usually she's pretty tense, all sharp corners, held-in energy. Now there was a kind of limpness, as if everything had been squeezed out of her. It scared me, but I knew that Gwen had probably made it very hard for her to come, I could see that sticking to her decision had exhausted her, and I didn't want to take that away by offering to forget the overnight part. But it was hard being with her, and it got harder. What I felt from her wasn't even childlike, a child who gets homesick and cries for Mama. She wouldn't cry, although the tears looked so close, just behind her eyes.

I'd decided that we'd shop for dinner together, get everything that she liked best and probably doesn't get. But in the supermarket she wouldn't choose anything. All I could get her to say was that she was tired, and she'd started wheezing by this time, so I picked her up, tall as she is, put her in the carriage seat, chosing the food myself. By then I was more than ready to give up. I said, 'Look Cleo, you don't feel good, let's just have dinner together. Then I'll drive you right home.' I expected her to brighten up, but she didn't. She just shook her head. After a lot of prompting she finally whispered, 'I can't.' I tried to convince her that of course she could, her mother would be glad to see her, but she just looked away, gasping, and wouldn't answer. I thought maybe she meant Gwen had gone out for the evening, but it seemed unlikely.

When we got home I said that we were going to call her house and speak to her Mama, but she shook her head again. I went ahead and called, but the phone kept being busy. All this time I could feel myself becoming less and less visible to her. By the time the food was ready she wouldn't let me touch her at all. Of course she didn't eat. I told her I was taking her home, which is when it really started. One of those tantrums like I'd seen her have at home, only much worse. She got totally hysterical, even wetting on the floor as she kicked and screamed. I grabbed onto her, held her as tightly as I could with all her kicking, and shouted that I was taking her home right now, although I had no idea how I could until she calmed down, there was no way I could carry her like that. At that point I realized that she was breathing very irregularly, hyperventilating. I remembered the attack which had alerted the department to Gwen and her family in the first place, when Gwen hyperventilated and passed out in the welfare office, and I got really scared. I was sure Cleo would pass out too, and maybe die. I kept trying to grab hold of her and she kept squirming away, and her breathing was getting more and more frightening. She still wasn't saying anything, but her eyes were terrified.

I finally managed to pick her up, and then she sank her teeth into my hand, an amazingly sharp, needle-like pain. I screamed and pulled her hair but she held on until she had to let go to try and breathe. I could tell she thought I was doing this to her, trying to take her breath away. I got a quilt finally, and rolled her up in it. Then I picked her up and got her into the car, where, thank goodness, she lay still and let me drive. She was hardly moving at this point anyway, getting the next breath was taking up every bit of her energy.

I drove her straight to the hospital, where they grabbed her up and started calling for doctors over the loudspeaker and yelling at me for waiting too long to bring her in and for not being her mother, because apparently they couldn't do anything to help her on my say-so. I finally got through to Gwen. She said she'd get a cab and be right there. When she did get there, about ten minutes later, with Anthony and Julius, she was calmer than I'd ever seen her, and more competent. She ignored me completely, went straight to the desk, signed the necessary papers, then disappeared behind the curtain, where they'd refused to let me go, to Cleo.

I stayed around for two hours or so until one of the nurses told me she was all right, but they were keeping her overnight because the attack had been so acute. Apparently she'd stopped breathing completely at one point. Gwen came out and I stopped her and tried to explain why I hadn't been able to reach her before, how sudden it had all been. She stared at me for a moment. Then she turned her back and walked away. I couldn't face going home, so I went over to Nicki's and collapsed there.

Early this morning I went in to see Cleo, and she was asleep, still wheezing pretty badly, making a whistling sound in her chest every time she breathed in. There was a transparent rubber nipple glued onto her bare chest, attached to a machine which registered her breathing pattern in electric blue lines, like the blue lines of the wave machine she liked so much at the aquarium. Cleo looked small and very brown among the white sheets in the big hospital bed. I sat down next to her, and after a while she opened her eyes. 'Mama, Mama,' she screamed. I left. I am nobody's Mama.

Gwendolyn, speaking

I was not surprised, was I Anthony? What I tell you before I put you to bed? I was up waiting. I was ready. They tell me I am too nervous, I imagine thing. Now they see who know true. I keep money in case something like this should happen, for a cab. Me and the kids arrive at the hospital in ten minute.

They tell me my baby stop breathing. The catbird she never even telephone me. She should thank she God if she got one that my baby is all right. That is one thing they will not take from me and go on to live. My children.

When I see my baby they have stick needles in her little arm. Rig she up to a big machine, try and make she

149

breathe. But nothing help until I get there, this what the nurse tell me. All rig up like she is, she hold she arm out to me. 'Mama,' she call, and start to breathe again.

SUPERBITY

Jo Jones

She gave her name as Jeannette, adding that she knew of
no surname. When pressed she gave that of her mother's
family. Much later, historians were to append her father's
surname, which she never did.

Her trial was held in a castle, but this is not the stuff of
a fairy story. Castles never were romantic places; only
their ruins are.

She wore the clothes of a young man. This is not the
travesty of a pantomime.

From its beginning the inevitable outcome of her trial
was death. She never believed for one moment that she
would be killed. She was not a martyr.

Before her trial she had been imprisoned for months
and moved from fortress to fortress as the turbulence of
war in the country made necessary. She had jumped some
sixty feet down from a tower window of one castle,
landing concussed and ill for a few days. At the trial she
was accused of trying to kill herself. Suicide was a grave
crime. She gave a variety of answers to the charge, always
refusing admission to despair. One answer was that the
war was faring badly in her absence, and she was
determined to return to it because her leadership was
vital. I trust this answer; it is of a piece with her sense of
importance. It also holds in it her confidence that she
could come to no final harm until she had finished what
she intended to do. She was not a martyr, not suicidal,

and never resigned.

Later on in her trial she asked to have the fetters on her legs removed. She was chained, and guarded night and day. The judges reminded her that she had tried to escape. She replied:

'True, but it is lawful for a prisoner to try to escape. I have not ever given my word not to try.'

She was less than twenty years old but had previously been taken to court charged with breach of promise in marriage, a case she had won. She must have shown then those qualities of being unswayed by argument and final in her statements. Girls had marriages arranged by parents, and consent was expected. Jeannette was not easily available for compromise.

She had run away from home. Her father believed that she would 'join the soldiers'. He had had a bad dream about her which could mean only one thing to him: that she would become a camp-follower. She may have dropped hints of wishing to be away and active in the war. He would understand this in only one way from a daughter. Her brother had been charged to keep a watch on her at home. He later joined her as a soldier when she had run away to become not a camp-follower but rather more than a paramilitary leader.

Her desire to go was not fanciful. She had seen the effects of war on the people of her own village where they lived in a state of passive fear of marauders, burning, destruction, and with the hostility of neighbouring communities with different allegiances. She was not a distanced genteel dreamer.

She had become, in slightly more than a year of visible action, rather more than anyone had bargained for. Her unwritten brief was to function as a figure-head and morale-raiser to a defeated and depleted army, the embodiment of emotional last-resort as in: God is with us, or historic inevitability is on our side. She was expected to sit on a horse, say confident words to the soldiers, and for the rest to behave impeccably.

She was by no means unique in her time. Several other women and a few men had sprung up from that stony ground of suppressed revolt, war and heresy, and flourished briefly as wandering leaders. It has always been a dangerous part to play.

Jeannette's task was to radiate sureness, spirituality, courage. Her downfall was that she was still sure, spirited and brave when those qualities were no longer called for. At this point she became a political embarrassment. She couldn't begin to understand that. Nor could she choose to step down from being the kind of woman she was.

Her trial was improperly conducted and a few men had spoken their doubts about it. They had fled the place because their remarks put them in great danger.

An official nodded to a clerk and a chair was fetched for her. The import of her trial gave her some short-term privileges. Around the time of the proceedings against Jeannette five other women in the same town stood for judgment on comparably open charges; three Joans, one Alice, and one Caroline, the red-head. They probably stood for the duration of their trials.

She wore the remains of expensive clothes, maybe the same ones she had worn when she had been pulled from her horse and captured. Her black hair was cut short. I'd like to think of her wearing the long robe over her dark clothes, a gift, patterned with nettle-leaves in pale green on dark, the vert-perdu or lost green which had taken the court's fancy and hers a season ago. I like to think of her vanity, her pleasure in fine clothes, her pride in being so good at spinning and sewing that she announced to the court that she could take on any woman from that town with her skills.

Her persistent refusal to give up male clothing and wear a dress had good reason and maybe much else to uphold it. Many women camp-followers dressed up as pages; it was practical and sexually charming. Definitively saintly women who set out to inspire wore dresses. The churchmen probed incessantly at her unwillingness to put on skirts. She said the time might come when she would, but she would say when. The records are incomplete but there have been persistent hints that the charge of gross impropriety held an unspecified charge of sexual aberration; mention was made of her preference for sleeping with young women rather than old. Sleeping with people of one's own sex was the custom of the time. I imagine that most young women would have preferred to share their beds with someone they could talk easily to and who would offer no worrying reminders of age. Besides, the purity of her body mattered so much to her that it is unlikely she would take more than a diffused pleasure in the closeness of another woman. As for men: she thumped one who tried to touch her breasts when she was being measured for clothes.

The hostile soldiers who guarded her could easily have raped her. Had they done so it is unlikely they would have suffered much as a result, but she would have lost her virginity in which so much of her validity before the court rested. Wearing male clothes may have helped her remain untouchable for so long. In the brief period when she gave way and put on a dress, she said in tears that she had been abused by her guards. There has not been so great change in the passing of years. Women are still preferred in skirts which leave them available. Safety rests on a male consensus not to take up that availability. When women wear trousers there is a preference in fashion for them to be tight and defining. The offer has to be made. Jeannette claimed control of her dealings with her sexuality, and doubled the demand by choosing how to dress herself. It happened to be astute for her survival: it answered to something else as well.

She named herself Virgin, choosing a particular word for that state which carried a teasing message, not like that of the Virgin Mary: it implied a young woman not yet sexually active but certainly in transit and not intending to become a nun. Her judges were confused. She gave them little certainty. She was accused of being subtle, as a woman is.

It is curious that her male dress was reverse-mirrored by the men around her. Many of them wore the cloth of the mother church, bride of Christ, the long skirts of priests.

What control over events she had was from her nature not from any mock-male stature. Standing five feet two inches tall, speaking a forthright country dialect in a light voice, of peasant family: she had to rely upon only the self which was in part those elements, but more her sureness in a splendid world of confirming voices which the men around her did not hear. It is as if when we think we were to be told: you did not think that. You are deluded. It seems a familiar predicament in an extreme form.

She had occasional days of peace, of a kind, confined in her room with guards while the judges argued over some answer she had given which had cut short their questioning. They were not used to being confounded by prisoners. Most who faced trial were awed by the cleverness of their judges, and crushed by the knowledge that argument or denial led only to the infliction of pain. Some resisted the admission of guilt in order to delay the sentence, maybe even believing that their innocence would hold against suffering. They were wrong. They came to welcome as gentle intimates the unarmed questioners who stood by and asked softly: tell me now. This woman did not, it seemed, understand the code of behaviour. What she did understand she over-rode. She did not see herself as guilty of anything and did not expect to suffer. Resignation was not a quality she had ever shown signs of understanding or having any patience with.

She spoke to her judges as if she had information to give them which would put right their wrong thinking. She spoke as if she expected release followed by honour. Her arrogance was like a cathedral door slammed in their faces. She resided in a good and truthful place, they were shut out in the darkness of error. Any humility she showed in the court was of no use to her. Her judges required the rape of humility which can mouth: I am nothing, know nothing, you know what is and what is true. Her arrogance was appalling to them. 'She answered well, notwithstanding the fragility of women' . . . 'She was very subtle, with the subtlety of a woman'.

She affronted them deeply. Women, it seemed, liked her; she was affectionate, intimate and talkative. Her life amongst soldiers, moving by night, sleeping out, discussing tactics and riding into battle, did not sever her natural likings as a woman amongst women. She cried easily and copiously: though it was often because she was affronted and the tears were of rage. To men she lacked the easy middle ground which women perceived. She begged for the company of a woman in her prison; it was normal for women to share company and bed. She was refused.

The many charges against her can be rolled up into one iron ball and hurled through the walls and bars of their prisons: superbity. It is their own word, here, catch. A blend of pride, arrogance, conceit, disobedience, indiscipline, critical intelligence, non-conformity, a refusal to bend the knee and give up the vision. Very little can be allowed for their sense of duty and order, tradition and political pressure. They were small. She was rampageous. She, others of her kind and those who have been forgotten are women to be glad of, a celebration.

Here are some of the words she said in that tight narrow room. In my own constricted place she smiles and opens windows to a scudding and dangerous sky, winds that toss dead order all over my room.

When she disliked a question she gave orders:

'Leave that. Move on.'

She refused to take a full oath to tell the full truth and argued that they might ask things which were nothing to do with the court and which she would not be willing to answer. Day after day she held out against the full oath.

'You may ask me such things that as to some I shall tell the truth, as to others, not.'

At the third hearing she said drily:

'There is a saying among little children that people are often hanged for telling the truth.'

Unfortunately she was not speaking to people who are childlike on the receiving end of authority, she was speaking to the law-makers.

She responded to direct questions with diversionary or irrelevant answers. These were techniques which dissident groups had developed and taught their members to use. Tactically they can delay or disable a court unprepared for the possibility that the prisoner will not obey their rules of conduct. There is no evidence that Jeannette had formative contacts with such dissidents but they had been active in northern and central Europe at that time. Maybe she was advised by her common sense, which was so heightened as to be uncommon. Perhaps her experience of language used by men in power, the traps they set, had taught her in her own good interests to refuse to step inside. Times have not changed in all respects. Certainly she was asked several compelling and dangerous questions: a yes or a no, or refusal to answer at all, each would have been damning.

The voices and presences which inspired her were those of saints of the catholic church. This was the time of Catholic Europe. Her stand cannot be dismissed because she was religious and not a member of a modern political party. Nor should anyone disparage the way in which she received her ideas, as personal, seen and heard. What matters is not how or why they came, but whether what she received from them made good sense. It did.

As a snare she was asked: did saint Michael appear naked to her? If she answered yes she was condemned as a whore. If she said no, further questions might lead to some detail of his clothing which could mark her as a follower of a demonic cult. The possible charge of witchcraft hung over her the whole time. To her military enemies it was the only charge they were interested in: she had defeated them in battle, so she must be a witch. It was not part of her final indictment, an extraordinary outcome since so. many minutiae could prove it. Not one of us would have escaped.

She replied sharply to the question of saint Michae''s sartorial preferences:

'Do you think that our Lord has not the wherewithal to clothe him?'

She found the query absurd and threw it back to the judges. It left them with a perilous nicety to consider; or to leave her alone.

She was asked if she was in the grace of God. It was a terrible and underhand question. If she said yes, then she was guilty of absolute pride and detached herself from the common fallen state of mankind. If she admitted no, then any further words of hers would be invalid, she was guilty and denied the saving grace of Christ's death. Her reply brought proceedings for that day to an early ending.

'If I am not, may God put me there, if I am, may he keep me there.'

The judges sent her back to her cell and thought long and hard how to deal with such a difficult woman.

I find it necessary to keep in mind the ideas, the unthought assumptions, the complex smothering weight of the procedures she faced; without this it is impossible to see the splendour of Jeannette standing against them in that room.

There were a large numbr of judges or assessors in the court, and a strong and hostile contingent of 'observers' from the leaders of the army opposing her and enraged by their defeats. They were not obliged to hold silent. They intimidated some of the questioners for failing to press home charges which would lead to a quick conviction. The judges were the jury. She had no counsel to defend her. She had no right to challenge prosecution witnesses. Above all, no charges were specified. She was open to a finding of guilt for anything she said as the days went by, or any evidence that came to hand. No charge was ever read or explained to her. A clerkly record was kept but there was no one to check it on her behalf. If she wanted to keep any control of what passed, she had to remember at the end of each day's disordered proceedings what she would need to think about in her cell ready for the challenges of the next day. The lingua franca of the courtroom was Latin, known to the scholarly men who tried her and to some observers. It was not a language available to Jeannette. Smatterings of English would be used among the observers. She knew no English. Her responses must have been discussed in front of her, sometimes in her own tongue but sometimes in languages she could not intelligibly query. She could not read or write. Only an élite, mainly male, could do so. There were a few courtly and highly literate women. One was Diane de Poitiers. She wrote later of Jeannette and held her in high esteem. Jeannette could not take notes. She was on trial for what she was as well as what she may have done, and was presumed guilty from the outset.

She was insensitive to the massive threat. She did complain that she grew tired and objected to the presence of male guards in her room. She remained sure of herself through all the weariness. At a certain point in the proceedings it was decided to limit the number of people present by retreating to a smaller room. She had an ascendancy over the mob in the court, just as she had on the battlefield. Things were not resolving themselves as church, state and soldiery required. Perhaps progress would be quicker if there were no shouters and no doubters.

They asked: what had her voices advised her in her room since the last session? Her reply was bald.

'That I should answer you boldly.'

They asked; she had answered. They asked whether (before the trial) she had letters asking her which claimant to the papacy should be obeyed? She said that she was busy when the letter came, and she had replied that she'd answer the letter when she had time. There is no mention of the judges querying her right to give a decision to this hierarchic question. In court she was asked: Which did she believe was the true Pope? No one cared for her judgment, but an answer could trap her. She threw the lethal question back.

'Are there two?'

They asked if she had seen or known by revelation that she would escape. She replied:

'That does not come in your trial.
Do you want me to speak against myself?'

Of course they did; she seems truly not to have realised that the case rested largely on catching her into damning herself by her own words. But they could not say so.

How much did she understand of what was going on? It is impossible to know. If she had somehow become familiar with this specialised form of legal discourse, then she handled it with a skill that transcended masters. If she did not then her own good wit was so tough and serviceable that it frequently reduced theirs to impotence.

A popular wandering preacher, Brother Richard, who pulled into his orbit several women with talents for inspirational speaking, had come to see her in the earlier days of her success. As he approached he made the sign of the cross and sprinkled holy water around the place to protect himself from harm should she prove to be a witch. She had watched wryly and said:

'Approach boldly. I shall not fly away.'

She found absurd any claims that she had special powers, heavenly or demonic, beyond the completion of her practical task. A sick nobleman had sent for her hoping for some miraculous cure. She looked at him, said she could do nothing, and advised him to go back to his good wife and leave his mistresses. She laughed when people clustered around to touch her.

The judges were eager to corner her into making claims as a miracle-worker. How a body which sanctified such people after their deaths could regard any living practitioner as implicitly damned is a quaint anomaly of history. But it was a time in which the extensive witch-hunting of the next two hundred years had its start. Europe had been ravaged by the Hundred Years War and the plagues of the Black Death; the social fabric was torn, sufferings widespread, and the desire for order and retribution of almost any kind as strong as was needed to counter the schisms and destruction. Yet executions for witchcraft and sorcery were a feature of the later 'enlightened' Renaissance, not of the Middle Ages.

The irony was that Jeannette was orderly and heirarchic in her thinking, in every respect save a wilful determination to do what she had decided. She expected her society in microcosm in the courtroom to accept the disruptive notion that as a female and an illiterate peasant she had a right to transcend her place in society. Moving by the analogic force of thinking, she had been reborn into a new caste. The new name she gave herself and her success in being this new woman proved her new nature.

At the very first hearing she had been told to recite the Pater Noster, Our Father. This was normally asked at witchcraft trials. The slightest slurring, hesitation or fumbling was taken as clear evidence that the devil was working through the speaker. Since the speaker also knew of this interpretation, and knew the results of failure, it was nigh impossible not to produce some falsity or slip in the saying. Jeannette countered the order to recite with: yes, she would, if she could say confession to the bishop first. When she was refused this, she in her turn refused to say the words. She maintained this refusal every time she was asked. Would she say the Pater Noster now? Yes, if she were allowed confession. Would she put on a woman's dress? Once she replied:

'If you give me permission, give me one, and I will take it and go. Otherwise no.'

Alternatively: yes, if she were allowed confession. There was total common sense in her refusal. She couldn't gain by agreeing to recite. She deeply desired to be confessed. But there was another consideration. She was treated as excommunicate before the trial even started. If she were allowed confession, then her judges would be admitting her, at least until the trial was concluded, into the body of the church and no longer into a limbo of guilt. The whole tenor of the proceedings would have been different.

She was finally given what she wanted. She was given it shortly before she was executed, well after she had been condemned as a heretic and cut off from the church. So she had then no right to it, another quirk of reasoning from the men of intellect.

She was quite capable of threatening her judges. At the third hearing she said to the bishop:

'Beware of saying that you are my judge. For you take on yourself a great responsibility.'

Later:

'You are putting yourself in great peril.'

At the eighth hearing, when asked if her saints had told her that she would be released from prison within three months:

'That is not in your trial.'

She added that those who wished to remove her from this world might well themselves go first.

In the setting of the times and the trial her confidence and pride were an outrage. The judges were often appalled and dimmed; they suffered shock.

When it was decided to move on to the formality of

showing her the instruments of torture with admonitions to admit guilt before they were used, she said words which still sound out over five hundred years:

'Truly, if you were to tear me limb from limb and make my soul leave my body, I could not say to you anything else. And if you force me to do so, then afterwards I shall say that you made me say so by force.'

They retired to cope with this. Contrary to practice, they decided by a majority not to use torture. The Master Executioner is recorded as saying many years later: 'On this occasion she answered with such prudence that all present marvelled. I retired without doing anything.'

The word these men used to express her total offensiveness was Superbity; unholy pride, arrogance, and an inflated mind. She had not conceded a single point to them.

There have been so many unknown women of courage and beauty who have lived and died unremembered. Some are shades around Jeannette; there was Pieronne who died in Paris just before she did, maintaining to the end Jeannette was right, that what she did was well done.

I remember Jeannette who laughed and cried so easily, who won the affections of so many women, loved fine clothes and expected to be honoured, who kept unshakeable loyalty when once she had given it; and in remembering her I find it possible to remember them all. If I knew their names I would sing them. They are reborn in every generation of women, they are alive now, as unmanageable as they ever were.

LET US NOW PRAISE UNKNOWN WOMEN AND OUR MOTHERS WHO BEGAT US

Sara Maitland

It was the apples that did it.

The smell of warm apples, because in the weary muddle of the evening before, she had left the bag of apples too near the radiator; and the memories, released, surged into the dark room and wrapped her as tenderly in their arms as she wrapped her baby.

No one had warned her, or rather, yes they had but she had not been able to hear any warnings. The utter exhaustion, the disorienting lack of sleep, the constancy of demand, those things she had more or less anticipated. But the debilitating draining passion of love she had not been prepared for; nor the sense of being laid too wide open, spread out too thin, her sense of personal boundaries destroyed, the confusion of self and other, the exposure of body and thought to the use of another and not even knowing when it had become another, not a part of herself. Worse, worse than being-in-love, an experience she had always found uncomfortable and self-annihilating, because the object and the source of the passion, the self-destruction and the confusion was both utterly vulnerable to her and utterly ungiving. She had woken and slept and listened and organised and suffered physically and slaved and poured out the resources of her own body, blood and milk and time and energy, for six unrelenting weeks of service to someone who gave nothing in return, nothing at all except the physical fact of its existence. The baby took, and took and took and took, long after she had nothing left to give and still she did not hate but loved the baby, passionately, tear-jerkingly and finally wearily, bitterly, defeatedly, and this was the third time in five hours that she had been dragged awake, her dreams smashed, fragmented, stolen, sucked down with the milk into the maw of that all-consuming, tyrannical, tiny, powerful, beautiful body.

And then she caught the smell of apples, and sitting on the dark sofa with her daughter sucking, sucking, sucking she spins away out across the galaxies of time and memory and smells afresh apples in a warm cupboard, tastes the strange cleanness of elderflower tea, touches the soft roughness of old linen curtains, hears the clear note of a flute playing in a next-door room, sees beautiful orange dragons on delicate china cups and knows herself, long legs in shorts, bony, awkward, lost, waylaid temporarily on her certain journey through childhood. Ten or eleven years young; unkempt, not physically but emotionally, lonely, fierce, on holiday with her mother and her mother's new lover; husband and child replaced. Husband rightly, the daughter knew, but herself *wrongly*, and dangerously and what certainty can there ever be again, and a great passion of anger and injustice and trying-to-be-good and sulking instead. And too much, 'why don't you go out and play darling?' and 'go on, darling, don't mope around so, the fresh air is good for you,' and 'do go out and enjoy yourself darling, you don't need to wait for us, we don't mind'.

So she had moped about through the first half of a hot and lovely country August. To amuse herself she took to spying on other people, listening to the chatter at the counter of the village shop, lurking behind the bus-stop and peering in through windows. She bought herself a note-book and filled it with mean sketches and vicious reports on all the people; and nobody liked her very much and none of the other children wanted to play with her because she was pretty horrid really. She speculated for her victims lives of dreariness and small mindedness and believed in the objectivity of her own observations so she did not even want them to like her, because they were horrid people anyway.

She extended her researches to the edge of the village. Up a small track there was a cottage with a long garden and behind the garden a wooded slope with undergrowth and one morning she decided to hide up there and see what she could see. A hot sunny morning, and the garden with rough grass, not a lawn, which ran under fruit trees and around casual flower beds down to the green back door. And after a little while a big, fat, old woman came out of the door and started weeding in the garden. She turned her back on the slope and leaned down to pull weeds, leaning from the waist with her legs apart, barely thirty feet away. And the enormousness of her bottom sticking up, the rest of her trunk and head invisible, huge and fat and disgusting, her floppy tweed skirt stretched wide and held by the huge knees, ungainly, ugly, and from the vantage point in the undergrowth spendidly ludicrous. So she whipped out her notebook and was about to sketch that enormous bottom and write some telling comments on it and its owner, when without looking up, and without turning round the gardening-woman said, very loudly, 'Don't you dare.' And without thinking she had shoved away the notebook and said, 'What?' 'Don't you dare write any comments on how hideous and silly I look here.' And the woman straightened up but still did not turn round, her hair was escaping wispily from its bun, and she still looked silly and ugly, her cardigan was baggy too. 'Come down here.' She had been frightened then, embarrassed and scared, convinced that the woman would demand to see the notebook; but she tried not to let it show, hopped over the garden fence jauntily, and with a moderately successful assumption of effrontery strolled down the garden. But the woman did not demand or ask anything, she just smiled and said, 'My name's Elaine, what's yours?' The smile undid her jauntiness, 'Clare,' she muttered, shifting from leg to leg. Elaine said, 'Well if my legs are too fat, yours are too thin. Do you like our garden?' and without touching her, she showed Clare round the garden telling her the names of the flowers, and pointing out interesting things that were happening – rose suckers and old nests and ripening fruit. She never mentioned the notebook. Emboldened Clare finally asked, 'How did you know? I mean that I was there, and about the notebook?' 'Oh, I'm a witch,' said Elaine calmly, 'my friend is too; and we have a cat as our familiar, who everyone thinks is called Smudge, but whose real name is Thunder-flower.' She was not laughing at Clare and Clare knew it. Elaine said, 'Why don't you come in and meet the others?' and they had gone quite comfortably through the green door and into the kitchen. From the front of the house she could hear a flute playing, and Elaine said, 'That's Isobel but she'll finish practising in a minute; in the meantime if you look in that cupboard you'll find three blue mugs. Could you get them out while I boil the kettle?' And while Clare was looking in the cupboard which was full of different coloured mugs and plates, not proper sets like her mother had but different colours and sizes, some of them old and fine, and some of them modern pottery and some just plastic, and getting out the three blue ones, the flute playing stopped and Elaine put her head out of the kitchen and called, 'Isobel, we've got a visitor.' Isobel, who was very tall and not much older than Clare's mother, but much messier and wearing the sort of crimplene slacks that her mother would not have been seen dead in, came into the kitchen and looked at her and said, 'How do you do?' not kindly to a child, but properly. She didn't seem to be at all surprised to see a strange child in her kitchen, but smiled and said to Elaine, 'I have had such a lovely practice, it was really sweet of you to go outside while I tried the frilly bits.' Then she reached down a tin from a high shelf and opened it and put it, half-full of biscuits, on the kitchen table. The kettle boiled and Elaine made the tea and she had sat with them at the wobbly table and they had chatted. And the women had asked no finding-out questions, they had just let her be and join in or not as she wanted. And when she realised that it was nearly lunch time she said that she ought to go and they took her through to the front of the house and let her out the front door very politely. When she was half-way down the path Isobel called out, 'We hope you'll be able to come again, any time you want to, drop in. You haven't met Thunder-flower yet.' And Elaine added, 'We need an apprentice anyway.' And when she got back to the cottage they were staying in she was not in a sulk any more, but she did not tell her mother where she had been all morning because she wanted to keep it as her own secret. She did not want her mother going and getting friendly with them.

And for the last two weeks of her holiday she went there nearly every day. They didn't do anything very exciting; they taught her how to make jam, how to care for the garden, how to store apples, each one having its own space and not having to touch the others. They gave her home-made elderflower tea to drink, a cool taste with a sharp touch somewhere, not like anything else she'd ever tasted. Isobel played on the flute and Elaine accompanied her on the piano and taught Clare how to turn the pages. Sometimes Elaine read stories to her and Thunder-flower coiled around her shoulders when she sat in the big armchair; and what they had done, though she did not know it then, was pay exquisite attention to her in the simple assumption that she was worthy of attention, that she was a nice and clever person, not a small and ferocious animal. So she told them lots of things that she had never told anyone else, and they listened and discussed them and were interested, but not pushy. She told them about school, and her friends at home and how she did not want to go and live in a new poky flat instead of her old house; she told them about the divorce, and how her father did not talk to people and was sad and grouchy, and about Ben who was nicer than that and how that made her feel bad, and about how angry she was with her mother and how she hated her and loved her and how it all hurt so much. And telling it aloud didn't make it feel better exactly but it did help it to make sense. They listened and respected her and liked her. She was too young even to wonder why, she was just happy and useful there with them and they were happy and useful with each other, and she could see that. It was true that they were witches and she knew it, although Isobel pretended to be a school teacher and Elaine pretended to be a retired school teacher, and Thunder-flower pretended to be a sweet little pussycat called Smudge; and if she had not known she would never have guessed that she came in from nightprowling with blood on her paws and wild green eyes. The flowers grew in their garden, the copper shone in their fire-place, the irregular weave of their curtains changed colour from minute to minute and the smell of apples pervaded the whole cottage. And one day when they had all been chopping up logs in the garden and Clare had helped carry them down to the wood-shed she saw their two broomsticks leaning against the shed wall and had felt a shiver of excitement. Two well-made besom-brooms, one slighter, thicker in the handle than the other and their delicate fingery twigs spreading out and casting tangly clear shadows from the afternoon sun on to the dusty walls of the wood-shed.

Her mother and Ben had been only too glad to have her

happier and calmer and busier, so they did not ask too many questions. The weight was removed and she flourished in the freer air. Once, when her mother had planned a well-intentioned and guilt-absolving picnic on the beach and Clare had casually rejected it in favour of one more day with Elaine and Isobel, her mother exclaimed in exasperation, 'Whatever do you do there all day? What's so special about two old ladies and a cat?' But Clare did not answer because she did not know. She was careful though, careful not to tell her mother they were witches, because a witches' apprentice never gives her teachers away. Sometimes they burned witches on bonfires, so she knew she had to be careful.

The holiday came to an end. She went the last day, sadly, to say goodbye to them, to try and say thank you for a gift she knew even then she had been given without knowing what it was. They had tea together, not in the blue mugs but in some beautiful delicate china cups with orange dragons on them; not at the kitchen table but in the sitting room, and although it was not cold they had lit the fire for her. There was cinnamon toast and fat fruit cake with nuts in. Isobel poured slowly, carefully, from a silver tea-pot. They had made tea special for her, ritualised, timeless because she was their friend. When it was nearly time to go Elaine had looked her straight in the eye and said, 'You know I think you should leave that notebook with us. You know we will never, ever read it, but we would keep it safe: furious, mean thoughts need to be kept safe. We will put a very firm, strong, good spell on it.' And she had taken it out of her pocket and given it to them without a qualm. Isobel said, 'Of course we will replace it for you.' They gave her another notebook, small and covered in bottle-green watered silk, and the pages were old and creamy, heavy, soft, and they had no lines, just blank so she could write and draw whatever she chose. It was ancient and beautiful. 'It's a spell book,' said

Elaine, 'You can of course put in anything you want, but try only to make strong, hopeful spells if you can. It is all right to do angry spells, but not mean ones or despairing ones. Remember – "Hope has two lovely daughters – anger and courage." Witches always take responsibility for what they do. They are loyal and loving and hopeful.'

'Have you made me a witch now?' she asked.

'No,' said Elaine, 'nobody can ever make anyone a witch, but you can be one any time you want to. You just have to believe it, that's all. You just say, "I am a witch" and you will be. You can even fly if you want to, but you have to believe in your own power. You see, it's very easy.' She smiled and Clare smiled back. 'Oh, and by the way, you don't need to have a broomstick, that's completely optional. All you need is to remember that you are a witch woman, full of power and strength and then you can do anything you want. You can make things and break things and call storms and grow plants and heal people and hurt people. It's up to you.'

And a little later she had gone down the path in the long light of the afternoon, leaving them standing arm in arm in their cottage doorway. She had been completely and perfectly happy, warm tea and toast in her tummy, warm love and power in her stomach. The next day she and her mother and Ben had driven away and she had gone back to school and forgotten. She had forgotten. But now, feeding her new daughter in the depths of the night, she remembered. She remembered not just the happenings of that summer, but absolutely the taste and touch and sight and smell and sound of them. She remembered her own nervous embarrassment when Elaine had called her from the garden; and how comfortable it had been with the two of them. She felt again how it was to be a perfectly and absolutely happy child, and knew again the power and goodness of being a strong woman.

So, now, she laid the sleeping baby on the sofa beside

her, and wedged her in with a handy cushion, because a witch always takes responsibility for what she does, and she walked over to the window and opened it. The moon, on its wane, rode the shoulder of a cloud and illuminated its frilled edges; the air was cool and milky. She said, 'I am a witch. I can make things and break things, and call storms and grow plants and babies and heal people and hurt people. I believe in my power. I can fly.' In her cotton nightdress she clambered on to the window sill and leapt out into the waiting air. After the first delighted surprise at finding that it really worked, she soared upwards, dancing upon the darkness, and testing her twists and turns. Steering was more problematic than she had imagined, but by no means impossible. She alighted briefly in the tree opposite her window to thank it for its beauty and generosity which she did not always remember to notice, then she flew back to the window to check on the baby. She was sleeping sweetly, the fluff on her head poking upwards and her long lashes folded downwards on her cheek. So Clare turned and left her and flew over London; a new strange and magical city seen from the air – Primrose Hill, a tiny paradise with little lampstands and the playground sheltering under the huge spider's web of the Bird House in Regents Park. St Pancras Station was a fairy-tale castle, turretting and cavorting outrageously in the moonlight, and the great dome of St Paul's a loving and protective breast. She swooped now, moving with certainty in her new element, and rose to greet the stars, and swung low over the streets of the City, deserted and ancient and longing for her visitation. She shot out over the river and flew upwards to watch it snake its glittery way across the town. She darted from side to side, delighting; the bridges were garlands, garlands of fire, linking the two heavier masses of earth across the deep of water; and the air embraced them all. She was perfectly and absolutely happy, and knew the power and the goodness of being a strong woman.

And as she flew down stream towards the docks and Greenwich she began to sing a deep new song, and she called on all other witches everywhere to come and sing it with her, and they came. Elaine and Isobel, still smiling, and a woman who lived four doors down from her at home and whose fierce purposeful striding had always filled Clare with fear; and the middle-aged woman who guarded the changing rooms at her local swimming pool and whose shiny black skin rippled gloriously in the moonlight; and the midwife who had delivered her daughter and hauled her through the confusion of pain and emotion. And more and more women, thrusting beautiful, confident bodies through the new air and singing, singing, singing her song with her. And flying over the river more fun than she could have dreamed: Formation Flying, as funny and silly and skilful as the women on *Come Dancing*; and Free Fall where there is no gravity but only perfect dignity; and Pairs, more sensuous and tender than terrestial dancing can ever approach; and Exhibitionism, solo flights and stunts of daring and careening wildness and mutual admiration; and just being there, flying, dancing with crazy immodest, hysterical, free laughter and song. 'Welcome to the Coven,' laughed a woman just below her and she looked down and it was her science mistress from school, who grinned and adjusted her white overall and not for the sake of decency. There were women she recognised from history books and portrait galleries and women she had never seen before, and young and old and in-between and witches' dancing skins come in more colours than the rainbow. And the trying soreness that still irritated her vagina from where she had been stitched after the birth was soothed and healed by the soft air, so she tugged off her nightie and laughed as it floated like a tiny pale cloud down into the river beneath. Turning deftly in the air she saw her stretch marks as silvery-purple bands of strength which glowed pearly in the moonlight. And she was full of joy.

And later she flew quietly home, leaving the radiant dancers, fliers, singers, because after childbirth a witch knows she needs a certain amount of quiet and solitude so that she can learn again what are her boundaries, and a certain amount of rest because caring for a small baby is very demanding; and witches always take responsibility for what they do. She rested after her pleasing exertions in the green tree outside her house and when she felt perfectly comfortable she flew back in through the window and alighted. Her daughter was still asleep, tidily on her tummy on the sofa, and the delicate hair which fringed the rims of her ears seemed to glow in the moonlight. Clare picked her up carefully and was about to carry her safely back to her basket in the bedroom when the baby opened her eyes, awakened but not frightened by the cool softness of Clare's naked body. Four eyes very close to one another and glowing in the dark like cats'. And the baby was so quiet, so present, so softly smelling of warm milk, so beautiful, so perfect, so courageous and bold a decision against such impossibly long odds, so little and funny, that Clare could not help but smile. She murmured, 'You little witch, daughter of a witch, you can be a witch too if you want to. Remember that.' And in the quiet of the ending of the night, the daughter, for the very first time, smiled back.

WOMAN OF LETTERS
A Life of Virginia Woolf
Phyllis Rose

Woman of Letters received considerable critical acclaim when it was first published in 1978. Now available as a Pandora paperback, Phyllis Rose's compelling biography assesses the way Virginia Woolf's past reverberates in her novels and places her feminism at the centre of her emotional and intellectual life.

Phyllis Rose tells the story of Virginia Woolf's life as Woolf herself might have perceived it; she revises the image of Woolf as an isolated technician unconcerned with social reality, giving us instead the picture of a woman immersed in issues that have become, if anything, more pressing since her death.

'Phyllis Rose writes with considerable insight and feeling of Woolf's attitudes to herself as a woman and of the possibility of being a woman writer.'

Margaret Drabble, *New Statesman*

'An admirable book'

Frank Kermode, *New York Review*

paper   £4.95   Biography/Life and Times
086358 066 1

MY MOTHER'S BODY
Poems by Marge Piercy

Marge Piercy's tenth book of poetry takes its title from one of her strongest and most moving poems, a harrowing tale of the need and confrontation in a mother-daughter relationship. Readers of Marge Piercy's previous collection (*Stone, Paper, Knife*) will not be surprised to encounter her mixture of the personal and the political. There are poems about doing housework, about accidents, dreaming, bag ladies, luggage and children's fears of the holocaust.

My Mother's Body is Marge Piercy's second collection of poetry to be published in Britain. It is her most moving and powerful collection.

Paper   £4.95   Poetry   086358 062 9
Pandora edition not available in the USA or Canada

THIS PLACE
Andrea Freud Loewenstein

'An energetic and passionate novel which grips the reader's attention with unholy force. It is an extraordinary evocation of a closed world – female bodies and female minds struggling against an imprisonment equally dire whether enforced or self-imposed, and written with charity and understanding.'

Fay Waldon

'Loewenstein vividly creates, through a naturalistic fidelity to voice and description, a stifling inferno.'

Michele Roberts

| Cloth | £9.95 | Fiction | 086358 039 4 |
| Paper | £4.95 | | 086358 040 8 |

CHARLEYHORSE
Cecil Dawkins

This is an explosive gallop through the family fortunes of mother and daughter on their huge ranch in Kansas.

Mother is a megalomaniac, daughter as stubborn as the bulls she manages; Cecil Dawkins' novel reworks traditional Western themes and is guaranteed to make you laugh, cry and see red.

Cecil Dawkins lives in New Mexico.

Cloth   £9.95   Fiction   086358 096 3
Pandora edition not available in USA or Canada

ORANGES ARE NOT THE ONLY FRUIT
Jeanette Winterson

'Like most people I lived for a long time with my mother and father. My father liked to watch the wrestling, my mother liked to wrestle. . .'

'The achievement of this novel is to make us squirm with laughter, then make us acknowledge how utterly sad it is when the needs of self-preservation turn what has been sacred into a joke.'

Roz Kaveney, Times Literary Supplement

'*Oranges* is a brilliant first novel – at once witty, gripping, imaginative and touching.'

Time Out

Paper   £4.50   Fiction   086358 042 4
Winner of the 1985 Publishing for People Prize for First Novel